The melody drifted hauntingly in the night

"I like your music," Steven murmured. Smiling, he pulled Lindsay down next to him on the couch, fitting her into the curve of his arm. Lindsay felt excitement begin to build, then stiffened under his caressing fingers. Love had been out of her life so long...she had forgotten how to follow it...forgotten, or else she was afraid.

"It's late, Steven. We have to work in the morning." She started to pull away, but he stopped her with a series of softly persuasive kisses along her throat.

"Don't go," he said huskily. "Stay with me tonight."

She knew she had to be honest with him. "Steven, I've been married...."

"I want you all to myself, Lindsay Hancock," he told her. "I don't want to share you with anyone—not even a memory."

Dear Reader,

We at Harlequin are extremely proud to introduce our new series, **HARLEQUIN TEMPTATION**. Romance publishing today is exciting, expanding and innovative. We have responded to the ever-changing demands of you, the reader, by creating this new, more sensuous series. Between the covers of each **HARLEQUIN TEMPTATION** you will find an irresistible story to stimulate your imagination and warm your heart.

Styles in romance change, and these highly sensuous stories may not be to every reader's taste. But Harlequin continues its commitment to satisfy all your romance-reading needs with books of the highest quality. Our sincerest wish is that **HARLEQUIN TEMPTATION** will bring you many hours of pleasurable reading.

THE EDITORS

U.S.
HARLEQUIN TEMPTATION
2504 WEST SOUTHERN AVE.
TEMPE, ARIZONA
85282

CAN.
HARLEQUIN TEMPTATION
P.O. BOX 2800
POSTAL STATION "A"
WILLOWDALE, ONTARIO
M2N 5T5

When Stars Fall Down

MEG DOMINIQUE

Harlequin Books

TORONTO • NEW YORK • LONDON
AMSTERDAM • PARIS • SYDNEY • HAMBURG
STOCKHOLM • ATHENS • TOKYO • MILAN

Published March 1984

ISBN 0-373-25102-5

Printed in Canada

1

A MARVELOUS SENSE of homecoming swept over Lindsay Hancock as she turned up the familiar lane and saw at the end of it her grandfather's barn cutting comfortably into the hillside.

But the place wasn't really the same. Her grandparents were dead now, and ten years had gone by since her last visit. The barn, once a shining white stable, had weathered to gray. Its loft opened onto a paved parking area instead of the paddock she remembered. And burned into the wood over the doorway was another sign like the one that had signaled her turn off the highway: STRAKE FARM WINERY. Below, in smaller letters, she read: *Visitors Welcome, Sunday Afternoon Tours on the Hour.*

It happened to be Saturday, not Sunday, but Lindsay parked her rented car and hailed a freckle-faced girl of about nineteen, who was emerging through the loft door with an armful of green bottles. "Could you tell me where I might find Mr. Strake?"

"Sure. Go inside and take the stairs down." The girl's wide mouth curved up in a friendly grin. "He's out back somewhere. Just give him a call."

The stairway seemed narrower than when Lindsay had raced up and down it as a child, and she picked her way carefully, her eyes adjusting slowly to the dusky interior. At the bottom she paused, greeted only by silence and a sea of silver dust motes drifting through the quiet air.

She moved farther into the room. "Steven Strake?"

"Out here." The voice, crisp and commanding, came back at once from the other side of a wide doorway through which horses had formerly pranced. "Bring me the wrench, will you?"

Lindsay saw that a concrete terrace had been added at the back of the barn and on it a man lay stretched flat beneath a piece of bright yellow machinery, his muscular legs in cutoff jeans protruding, his face and most of his body hidden.

A wrench, he had requested.

Lindsay turned back to scan what had once been the tack room, acutely aware as she looked it over, of the absence of bridles and harnesses, and of the sterile presence of a row of stainless-steel tanks flanked by dozens of wooden barrels. No hay. No stalls. A painful wave of nostalgia thickened her voice as she called back toward the terrace, "I don't see a wrench."

She heard an impatient snort. "Look under your nose. And hurry, can't you? The blasted thing is jammed and dripping all over me."

Lindsay took another look around and finally located the tool in a crate where someone had tossed it along with some greasy rags and an assortment of stained corks.

On the terrace she put the wrench into a waiting, purple-splattered hand and stepped back. The machine, she saw, was a grape press. The voice that had snapped at her turned cheerful and curious. "New shoes, Katie?"

"I'm not Katie." She shifted her high heels on the gritty concrete. "I'm Lindsay Hancock." A late-September breeze stirred her hair. "I've come about a job."

The wrench clanged purposefully against the underside of the press. "Sorry, Lindsay Hancock. There aren't any jobs."

"*The Terrapin Times* says you're hiring."

"Then you're looking at last week's issue."

Lindsay brought the folded newspaper from beneath her arm and saw with dismay that he was right. Coming out of the inn with it, she hadn't noticed the date. She had been too intent on the purple haze the Connecticut hills wore, their loveliness bringing a lump to her throat, reminding her vividly of other autumn days when she had cantered joyously through leaf-speckled lanes and then come back to the farm for cold milk and sugar cookies still warm from her grandmother's oven.

It hurt her to think of the horses, too. Cinder and Sunrise. Miss Mattie Bell and Quicksilver. Even their comforting animal smells had given way to the acrid odor of grape squeezings and of withered stems piled high at the edge of the terrace. In town, her grandparents slept beneath a hundred-year-old beech, and the farm she had loved as a girl had been converted into a vineyard by this man who hadn't even the courtesy to roll out and have a look at her.

"I want a job here," she announced flatly. "There must be something I can do."

He did roll out then. He locked his arms around his knees and gazed up at her with a penetrating stare that took in admiringly the sweep of dark hair that fell over her shoulders. He gazed at her smoky eyes and her piquantly curving lips and pointed chin. "What's your background?"

"Four years at Boston U and two years on the West Coast. But I don't expect my experience or my degree to apply here."

"Why not?"

She found it difficult to speak seriously to a man whose craggy face was splotched with grape juice, but it was a serious moment for Lindsay and she divided her attention between his unwavering blue eyes and a chin that looked as solid as the Rock of Gibraltar. "I majored in music." Without knowing she was going to, she added, "I write songs."

He gave her an engaging grin. "Sing one for me."

"No—" But the grin was contagious and she smiled. "This is a job interview, not an audition."

"There aren't any jobs. Besides, pickers were all I was hiring." His interested gaze traveled over the fashionably cut blazer that buttoned snugly at the waist of her scarlet skirt. "You're overqualified for that."

"For picking grapes?" She had seen the sun-warmed clusters from the car as she drove up. Rows and rows of them, dangling from vines that stretched past her grandfather's white clapboard house and dropped off into the valley that was providing a backdrop now for the self-assured stranger staring at her. She pictured herself moving along the vines, sunlight on her shoulders, the crisp, Connecticut air filling her lungs. "I don't mind being overqualified."

"All the jobs are filled."

"*Please.*" The instant she heard the urgency in her voice, she regretted ever having turned off the highway. She didn't have to beg. In her purse were letters of introduction to a producer of off-Broadway musicals. When she had left California, the studio where she had been composing commercially for television told her the door would always be open. It was stupid to have come back. Everyone knew that you can't go home again.

Yet here she was.

She swallowed and brought her chin up. "Never mind. I'm sorry to have troubled you."

"No trouble." He gave her a quizzical look and got up, unfolding with easy grace until his wide shoulders were even with the top of her head. His body was long and lean, and Lindsay saw how tanned and athletic-looking his legs were. Probably he was a runner. An unruly thatch of straight blond hair angled across his forehead, and the bright blue eyes she found so disconcerting looked out at her from beneath a jutting brow.

He said, "If you hadn't come along, who would have brought me the wrench?"

"Katie, I imagine." For some reason she had expected a much older man. How old was Steven Strake? Thirty, thirty-five? There were crow's feet at the corners of his eyes and laugh lines putting his sensuous mouth in parentheses. In spite of his maturity, he had a boyish appeal that drew her to him. But there was something in back of his eyes, too. An aloofness that told her he was more than an affable Connecticut grape farmer.

He cocked his head. "Why does a songwriter want to work in a winery?"

She took a stab at an idea that had been forming in her mind. "Why does a Harvard engineer want to own one?"

"Because he likes good wine, of course." The

answer came swiftly, smoothly, but it was obvious that her retort had startled him. "Anyway, it wasn't engineering. It was law."

"Which makes your choice even more intriguing." She could see that he was attracted to her, too, and her heart did an odd kind of flip-flop. "Harvard lawyers get instantly rich, don't they?"

"In ninety-nine instances out of a hundred, I'm told."

"Were you the unhappy exception?"

"I was successful enough to buy this farm and equip it." The aloofness took over. "What about you? Doesn't songwriting pay?"

"At the moment I'm not particularly interested in money."

His grin came back. "My, how noble and high-minded. You sing for your supper, I suppose."

They stared at each other and then suddenly Lindsay laughed, unable to deal in any other way with the bubbling excitement his gaze inspired. "I'd be willing to today. I missed lunch."

"So did I." He cast a sideways glance at the shiny press at his side. "Lilliput, here, got to leaking."

Lindsay glanced at the gleaming piece of machinery. "Isn't it supposed to?"

"Yes—but evenly. Not out of only half a dozen holes and then just when it wants to."

"Is Lilliput the name of the manufacturer?"

"No." He grinned again. "It's my personal term of endearment. It was the only word out of the manufacturer's instructions that looked familiar to Clint and me when we started to put her together." He ran his hand affectionately over the yellow paint. "She's French, and marvelously simple actually, but she arrived knocked down to cut the duty costs, and we had a devil of a time figuring out where her arms and legs went."

"Too bad I wasn't here." Lindsay tossed her hair back over one shoulder. "I read French very well."

His grin deepened the creases around his mouth. "Technical French? The language of Voltaire isn't quite the same lingo as industry uses."

Lindsay's eyes met his. "And of course you read Voltaire."

"Of course."

They were silent for a moment, taking each other's measure again. Lindsay decided that he was even more compelling when he wasn't smiling. She liked the shape of his hands. She liked the resonant tones in his voice, and it intrigued her that he had given up practicing law to wear cutoff jeans and have his face dripped on by a machine he had given a name to. Not that young men abandoning their professions for something more enjoyable was all that uncommon these days. But this man struck her as too disciplined for switching careers. He looked to her like a person who would have known since he was ten that he wanted to be a lawyer . . . or a winemaker.

Startled, she heard him chuckle. "What are you doing?" he asked. "Counting the hairs in my eyebrows?"

"Mercy, no." She held on to her poise though she felt a perfect fool. "I'd never get finished if I were doing that, would I?"

"Ah, a woman of wit. Where have you come from? Mars?"

"No place so exotic, I'm afraid." Regaining her composure, she looked back across the valley. "As a matter of fact, I grew up about thirty miles from here."

"Where?"

"At Christmas Church. Have you heard of it?"

"It isn't there anymore, is it?"

"No." Her throat tightened. Mention of Christmas Church always reminded her that there was no place left in the world that she could really call home. "There were only half a dozen houses to begin with and all of them burned."

"An explosion, wasn't it?"

Lindsay nodded. "A fuel truck passing through town collided with a train."

He studied her pensively for an instant. "Was anyone in your family injured?"

She shook her head. "My parents had moved away by then."

"What about you? Were you living there?"

"No." The fire had occurred the summer after she married Winston. They had an apartment near Long Island Sound and Winston spent his afternoons on his boat or lounging around the yacht club. In the evenings while she worked at home at the piano, he sat in the club's bar, smoking and playing poker with his friends. Probably he was sleeping with Sybil, too, but it wasn't until spring that she found out about that. She focused again on the deep-set eyes that were still studying her.

Suddenly Steven Strake was businesslike, anchoring his hands on his hips, giving orders. "It's quitting time. We'll go over to my house and scratch up something to eat and then maybe we'll talk about a job."

Lindsay blinked, her pulse quickening. "You said there weren't any."

"None that I feel like advertising. But one of our crew recently married and he's asking for more time off. Besides, it's hard to pass up an applicant who speaks French." His blue eyes twinkled. "If she speaks it very well, I have an idea it might be downright impossible."

2

THE HOUSE was much as Lindsay remembered it, except that the white Priscilla curtains were gone from the windows and the furniture was different. There was the wide hall one entered from the porch. The parlor stood to the left, the dining room to the right. In Steven Strake's dining room, the table was piled high with books. There were books everywhere, but most of them, she saw, were about wine, not the law.

He led her straight back to the kitchen. From the clutter that abounded there, it was apparent that he spent most of his time in that large, old-fashioned room. It had always been her favorite, too. Homey, comfortable, sunny. But now the shadows on the wide plank floors were lengthening, and Steven lighted the lamp that hung over the table before he brought out a bottle of white wine and two glasses.

"This was racked only this morning." He poured her glass a quarter full. "You're the first to taste it."

He watched with an appreciative glint in his

blue eyes while she swirled the clear liquid and then brought it to her nose for a tentative sniff. "Light," she said approvingly. "And it has a lovely floweriness."

He nodded, pleased. "It's a Riesling. We think it's just right for wedding receptions and those garden parties ladies love."

Lindsay lifted her glass to her lips and sipped. "Very nice." It was better than that. It was wonderful. It was smooth going down, and in her mouth it left a pleasant fresh taste that called for more. But if she praised it too much, he might think she was buttering him up for the job. Suddenly she was wary about working here. Steven Strake was too attractive . . . she felt much too at home in his kitchen.

He poured a glass of wine for himself and sat down in the chair next to her. "You've told me you write songs. Tell me what else you do."

Sidestepping his request, she urged, "Taste the Riesling. Aren't you dying to know if it's as good as you think?"

He gave a rueful smile. "I'm doing my best to give the appearance that it really doesn't matter."

"Why? To impress me with your savoir faire? I'm already impressed with Voltaire. Here—" Laughing, she raised the glass and put it to his lips, aware at the same moment that it was too intimate a gesture to make with a stranger, but unable somehow to stop herself. She was too eager to see his reaction. She wanted to see what would happen to those remarkable blue eyes when his marvelous vintage filled his mouth.

She wasn't disappointed. The blue deepened. He forgot she was there, concentrating all his attention on the miracle that had resulted from his skills as a *vigneron*.

"If this were an actual tasting," she teased, "I'd expect you to spit that out."

He swallowed instead, plainly relishing every drop. And then in a motion subtle and swift, he leaned across and planted a kiss full on her lips.

Shock tingled through Lindsay. The taste of the wine was still on his mouth, still on his tongue. It mingled with the woodsy, male scent of his skin against hers and a thrill ran up her backbone. He was interested enough in her to test the waters...and like herself with the wine, he had been too eager to wait.

His firm, plundering lips, certain of what they were about, turned on hers for another instant. Then he drew back and looked at her.

Lindsay returned the look, her smoky eyes telling him nothing, though in her lap her folded hands trembled.

"Good wine and a beautiful woman," he murmured huskily. "An unbeatable combination."

Lindsay's defenses rallied. "An unbeatable

package deal from Strake's Farm Winery. Isn't that what you mean? A sip of your latest Riesling and then a kiss to send it properly on its way."

Her bantering tone struck a note of discord in the quiet kitchen. He gazed at her evenly. "I suppose a good bit of wine is drunk in that sequence."

"I suppose it is." She passed the tip of her tongue over her lips, conscious that they still bore the imprint of his. Obviously the kiss he had given her meant nothing to him, either, and that suited her fine.

But watching him lift his glass again, she felt oddly let down.

They ate soon afterward. Lindsay stayed at the table like a proper guest, and Steven brought out of his refrigerator a hearty stew that he heated and served with crusty French bread, more wine and a chunk of Brie.

They talked. He was self-made. But she had already figured that out. He had put himself through Harvard on scholarships and part-time jobs. His father was a retired millworker living in one of the little towns that lay along the Massachusetts coast between Boston and Salem. Steven had four sisters, all of them older and married and living lives of their own in different parts of the country. His mother was dead.

"My parents are both living," Lindsay volunteered, but she wondered as she spoke whether the word really applied in their case. They were playing at life, in her opinion. Boating, swimming, sitting at bridge tables, or sunning themselves half the day on Florida beaches. Tensely idle was the way she thought of them whenever she visited, but she always rebuked herself afterward, afraid that it was Winston's hedonism that had warped her view of people having a good time. She needed to think more of how hard her parents had worked when they lived in Christmas Church and then afterward when they moved to Boston primarily to give Lindsay the advantage of better schools. They deserved the pleasure-filled life the sale of the Hancock farm had provided them. If she missed the farm and her parents in her own life, the problem was hers, not theirs.

Steven, seeing how solemn she had grown, offered a glass of a second wine he had brought out at the end of the meal. A dessert wine, sweet and a little cloying, Lindsay thought, and she only sipped hers. It was from a New York vineyard. A very good vintage, Steven said, and she made no comment, weary suddenly of having an opinion about everything, of being bright, smart Lindsay Hancock, independent and saucy, needing no one.

She remembered Steven's kiss and pushed back from the table. "If you'll excuse me, I'll be on my way. Thanks for a lovely supper."

Steven stayed seated, but he put out his

hand and caught one of hers. "You were supposed to sing for it."

"I kissed you instead." She meant to sound
flippant, but her voice came out a throaty
whisper and sent a streak of alarm cartwheel-
ing through her. With Winston she had never
been assertive in a sexual way. He had hated
her growing self-containment. The last of the
great white glaciers, he had accused toward
the end. Yet here tonight with a man she
barely knew, she was apparently sending out
signals, and it was obvious he was picking
them up.

His hand closed over hers, making her feel
wonderfully safe and desired, and at the same
time, in peril. He said, "We haven't discussed
your working here."

"It was a stupid idea. Forget it." But she sat
down again because it was awkward trying to
leave while he had a hold of her . . . awkward
to stand above him and feel his eyes moving
over her. "I haven't mentioned the real reason
I came. My grandfather owned this farm when
I was a child. I've been a little homesick lately.
I thought I'd come back." She tossed her hair
away from her face. "But it wouldn't have
worked out. I can see that now. I'm lucky that
you weren't hiring."

He took in her clipped sentences with no
change of expression. If he had been a trial
lawyer, she thought, juries must have wondered what to make of him.

"Why didn't you tell me that at first?"

"What difference does it make that I didn't?"

"It makes me feel that you don't trust me."

"I've just met you."

"Isn't that how relationships always begin? People meet; they like each other." His eyes followed the outline of her mouth and then lifted to meet her gaze head-on. Then suddenly his smile flashed, contradicting the seductive pressure of his thumbs gently massaging her knuckles. "Before you go, at least tell me what the place was like when you used to come here."

Lindsay began to talk of her childhood hesitantly, but it took her until nine o'clock to finish. Flattered by the attentive way Steven Strake listened, she kept remembering things. In autumn, the gaudy scarlets of the woodlands... the white-tailed deer and the snowshoe rabbits that crossed the bridle trails. In spring, blue fields of lupine, and later the wild roses tangling over the hedgerows. She remembered her grandfather notching his maple trees; the smell of apples filling the barn loft, bread rising in pans on the kitchen counters.

A clock struck in the hall and she jumped to her feet. "Good heavens! I've been boring you for hours!"

He stood beside her, stretching lazily. "I haven't been bored. I've been thinking while you talked that nothing much has changed. The man who bought the farm from your parents after your grandfather's death planted the grapes. I suppose he sold the horses, too. In my own turn, I've made the barn functional for processing the juice and bottling the wine, but the woods are still filled with the same sorts of animals. The leaves still turn scarlet and gold every autumn."

Lindsay nodded. "I'm the one who's different. I could never fit in here again."

"You won't know until you try."

"I'm not sure I want to try."

"You seemed sure enough earlier. What's changed your mind?" He was laughing at her. "Me?"

She said stiffly, "What would I do here if I stayed?"

"You offered to pick my grapes."

"And you said you didn't need pickers."

He shrugged. "I didn't when I counted this morning, but I hire transients to help out during the harvest season. One of them could fail to show up on Monday."

"What if he does show up?"

He shoved his hands into his pockets. "Then you can sweep the floors. You can run the machine that stems the grapes."

"Who's doing that now?"

"Whichever one of us is handy. That's the way we operate. On a regular basis there are only four full-time employees. Clint Phelps, Katie, whom you met, Rachel Byrd from the next farm, and myself. I'm in charge. I'm the winemaker. I make all the major decisions, too. But in all other respects we're a team, doing whatever needs to be done at the moment. That's the only way a small business like this keeps its head above the water. When the season gets into full swing we may have to work in shifts around the clock. Other days we may all go skiing."

It sounded charming to Lindsay. As comfortable as a family. Industry on a small scale with no pressure while she let herself soak up the changing colors... the gradual arrival of winter... while she learned again who she'd been before Winston's unfaithfulness and biting disrespect for her talent had made her cynical, wary and icily self-reliant. After the divorce she had fled to California where she had managed to thaw a little. But on this Connecticut farm, the only place she could remotely call home, she hoped she could rediscover a joy in life. Then she might be ready for New York, ready to write the kind of prize-winning scores Broadway musicals were famous for.

Steven's voice cut in. "I ought to warn you about one thing though. Since you're small, you'll catch a lot of tank duty."

"What do you mean?"

"You saw those stainless-steel tanks in the barn, didn't you? Every time they're emptied somebody has to crawl inside and scrape the collection of tartrates off the sides. It's a hell of a job." He grinned. "The only thing that makes it bearable is breathing the wine fumes in such close quarters. Sometimes you get a free high."

"Or pass out, I'd imagine!" Lindsay had once or twice suffered from mild claustrophobia. She couldn't see herself crawling inside a tank!

Steven read her thoughts. "Does the idea scare you?"

"A little." But if freckle-faced Katie could do it, why shouldn't she be able to? "I suppose I'd get used to it."

He folded his arms across his chest. "Are you saying yes to my offer?"

She stared at him for a moment. And then her smile broke through. "I guess I am."

"I'm glad." His pleased look sent prickles of excitement tingling up her spine. "The wages aren't much," he went on. "Sometimes I can only pay in company stock." His blue eyes twinkled. "But fortunately you're not interested in money."

"I hope I'll make at least enough to pay for my keep." She'd need to look for an apartment nearby. Something small and cozy, something snug against the New England winds. Her excitement grew. She was back in Terrapin Falls for better or for worse. Sweeping floors, stemming grapes. With a Harvard lawyer for her boss. In California they'd find that terribly amusing.

"Where are you staying now?"

"I have a room booked for tonight at the inn. But if I'm going to work here, I'll have to find something less expensive. It may take me through Monday to get settled."

"I doubt if you'll find anything in town." He carried their dishes to the counter and began running hot sudsy water into the sink. "You'd be lucky to locate a vacant squirrel hole in Terrapin Falls."

"Why is that?" Through her surprise, she noted the strong lines of his back tapering to an intriguing leanness at his hips. "There used to be dozens of dear little ladies who rented rooms."

"There still are. By the score. But there's a hydroelectric plant coming up along the river. The construction crews are spilling into every village around."

Lindsay's heart sank. Now that she'd made up her mind to stay, how awful if she couldn't! "What do you suggest I do?"

"You could stay here if you want."

His proposal stunned her. An entanglement with someone of the opposite sex was the last thing she needed! Even more to the point, if she had led Steven Strake to believe that she was the kind of woman who would be interested in sharing quarters after one kiss, she had a lot of backtracking to do! But he spoke again before she had time to decide how to go about it.

"Before Clint was married," Steven said,

"he was staying in a cottage at the bottom of the hill. It's not much. Four rooms. But it has a stone fireplace, and it's a tight little building. You ought to be fairly comfortable there. Best of all, it won't cost you anything."

"Does it belong to the farm?" Lindsay was too relieved to recall whether or not such a cottage had existed in her time.

"It was built for the vineyard keeper, I believe." Steven turned around with a wry grin. "Hopkins, the man I bought the place from, had rather grand ideas. But it came in handy for Clint. We can go and have a look at it if you like."

"Now?" She hoped she didn't sound too anxious.

"Why not?" He dried his hands and then ran them back over the straight blond hair that kept falling over his brow. "I'll get a flashlight."

She used the time he was gone to close the cabinets he had left standing open, and to dry the drainboard and hang the soggy towel evenly on a rack beside the sink. The place was scrupulously clean, but it was obvious from the disorder on the shelves and the number of books and unopened mail lying about that a man was in charge. Lindsay had never thought of herself as particularly domestic, but this was her grandmother's kitchen, and her fingers itched to put it to rights.

Reentering, Steven observed her with a wry

look. "I know what you're thinking. I need a housekeeper. Maybe I'll add that to your duties."

"I wouldn't mind." She smiled back at him, feeling secure now that she knew, for the moment at least, that her future was settled. "I love this house."

"So do I." He took her arm and opened the back door. Before them, the valley lay bathed in moonlight. Steven took one look and tossed the flashlight into a wood box. "We won't need that with a harvest moon, will we?"

The moonlight thrilled Lindsay, and as they moved along beside each other between the rows of grapevines, she felt renewed and purified by the clear white light falling over everything. After a few minutes she commented quietly, "I've lived in a city so long I'd almost forgotten how a full moon can look."

"So had I by the time I took over the winery." He had pulled on a sweater at the house, but he still wore his cutoff jeans, and Lindsay wondered as she watched him striding along why the chill night air hadn't turned his muscular legs into icicles. "I never intend to live anywhere again that prevents me from stepping out of my back door and looking at the stars."

"You haven't said where you practiced law."

"In Manhattan. At Dexter, Brink and Dexter."

It was a well-known firm. Corporate law

was their specialty and they were prestigious enough to have their pick of the country's law schools. "You must have been good."

"I was." His matter-of-fact tone held no hint of arrogance. "They made it hard for me to leave."

"Were you thinking about wine then, or were you just dreaming of the country?"

"Both." He guided her around a stack of baskets at the end of a row, and then she saw the cottage ahead, moonlight icing its roof. Shutters framed two high front windows and a dark door stood below in the middle. Absurdly, in Lindsay's mind the three composed a face, two eyes and a mouth, as friendly as a picture in a child's coloring book, and instantly she loved the place.

Steven brought a key from his pocket. When the door was opened, he flipped a light switch and out of the darkness sprang a living room, bedroom, bath, and kitchen. All four rooms were visible from where Lindsay stood on the threshold, delight shining in her eyes.

"Why, it's straight out of Mother Goose!"

Steven laughed. "Rub-a-dub-dub, three men in a tub?"

"I was thinking more of a gingerbread house." She hurried around the main room, casting admiring glances over everything. "Behold my parlor!" She clasped her hands together. "It's perfect, Steven! I've never seen anything as quaint as this furniture."

"It came out of Cracker Jack boxes," he joked, but she could see he was fond of it. "I inherited it from my mother's family. One of her uncles was a self-taught cabinetmaker. In his time off from the mill, he put furniture together as a hobby."

Lindsay went into the bedroom and came out again, exclaiming, "How can you bear not to have all these wonderful things in your own house?"

Every piece of furniture had its own personality, unobtrusive but distinctive when one focused directly on it. Even the drawer pulls were whimsically carved. The sofa where Steven had sat down resembled nothing so much as a bowlegged plump person waiting for tea. A pudgy, conscientious-looking table in the corner held a lamp. One chair was a serene rocker. Another one opposite it was shaped like half a barrel, rotund and pompous.

Steven grinned at her excitement. "The scale is a bit small for me, don't you think?"

She saw then that his knees were practically touching his chin and she collapsed in a fit of laughter on a calico-covered stool. "You look ridiculous sitting there!"

"Thanks a lot." But he shared her amusement. "I think Clint might have married just to get out of here before crippling deformities set in."

"Whatever his reason, I'm certainly grateful. I can't wait to move my things in!"

"When do you want to?"

"Tomorrow if it's all right." She jumped up to inspect the kitchen. "And tomorrow night, you must come to supper."

He got up languidly and followed her, standing with his hands in his pockets while she peeped into the bare cupboards. "What will you feed me?"

"Chicken Something-or-Other." She closed her eyes and blew dust off a shelf. "I'm very good with chicken."

"Is that so? Very good with French, very good with fowl."

She heard the irony in his tone and glancing up, caught his speculative look. "I don't mind bragging about myself, do I?"

Her abashed gaze softened his expression. "I don't call it bragging if you're telling the truth."

"Then I'll just have to prove that I am, won't I?"

"Not for me. I believe you. But just the same, I'll hold you to your offer. Chicken Something-or-Other sounds irresistible."

Suddenly to Lindsay the air seemed charged with electricity. Steven had made no move to come nearer, yet she felt herself drawn to him. It flashed through her mind that she wouldn't object if he kissed her again. The moment seemed to call for it, the way certain occasions demanded a toast.

She spoke with a slight catch in her voice.

"Thank you very much for providing me with this house."

"I'm glad it was available."

"I'll bring over my things in the morning."

He glanced again at the empty shelves. "You might need a few pots and pans."

"I have them." When she and Winston broke up housekeeping, she had stored their accumulation of domestic paraphernalia. Wedding presents, most of them. Some of them had never been out of their boxes. "I left a U-Haul at the inn."

Surprise flickered in the look he gave her. "You did plan to stay, didn't you?"

"Yes." Why did she feel as if she had tricked him? "If not here, somewhere nearby."

"For old times' sake?"

She brought her chin up, annoyed that it trembled. "For getting my bearings."

His gaze traveled over her. "I wish you luck then." In a minute she heard him going out the front door. "Take all the time you want looking around," he called back. "I'll be outside looking at the stars."

3

TOWARD THE END of the week as Lindsay took stock of her situation at the farm winery, she decided that except for one thing she had never been so relaxed and at ease.

It delighted her that the other members of the team Steven had described were so easy to get along with. It seemed as if she had known them forever. Katie, of course, she had liked the first time she saw her. At nineteen, the girl viewed the world as full of endless possibilities, and she sang all day in a pretty, clear soprano.

Clint Phelps, married for only six weeks to fragile blond Dorothy, whom he had known for only six weeks before that, moved around in a kind of blissful daze. Hired primarily to keep the machines running, he spent half of his time looking for the tools he had scattered all over the barn. Lindsay was fairly certain he was responsible for the "lost" wrench on the day of her arrival. But she discovered that when he put his mind to his work, he had the talent to fix anything. In addition, he had a shy charm and an endearing way of blushing to the tips of his sun-bleached hair whenever anyone mentioned his newly married state.

Rachel Byrd, whom Lindsay had expected to be in her twenties, turned out instead to be a grandmother. Afflicted by boredom after her children left home, she had started looking around for something to do at about the same time Steven Strake said goodbye to Dexter, Brink and Dexter. It was easy to see that Steven relied on Rachel's maturity and good-humored persuasiveness to keep the two younger members of the team operating at peak performance. Her crisp admonishments were more effective than anyone else's in rousing Clint from his marital reveries, and it was her talent for efficient organization that bridled Katie's boundless energies and channeled them in productive directions.

As for herself, Lindsay had everything to learn, and she was grateful that it was Rachel who was her teacher.

The older woman asked few questions when Lindsay turned up on Sunday morning, pulling a U-Haul behind her rented car and inquiring where the road was that led down to the cottage. Steven was nowhere about, and Rachel, dressed for church but conscientiously checking on the appearance of the barn before the afternoon tours began, had been the only one on hand to greet her.

She accepted Lindsay's brief explanation of why she was there as easily as if new members were added daily to the small staff. Then she climbed into the car and showed Lindsay the entrance to the two-track lane that skirted the vineyard and came to a dead end at the rear of the cottage.

Rachel had offered to stay and help Lindsay unload, but Lindsay had insisted she go on to church, promising that if she needed help, she would rout Steven out.

The next morning Rachel had introduced her formally to Katie and then to Clint and set her to work labeling bottles. Alone in the partitioned-off corner of the barn where a fascinating bottle corker was located along with the labeling device, Lindsay had plenty of time to let her thoughts drift.

Everything that occurred to her as she worked pleased her, but her memory of the evening before with Steven as her supper guest brought more pleasure than anything else. Throughout the morning she'd kept coming back to it.

The meal she had prepared for him had been a resounding success. A steady procession of visitors had toured the winery in the afternoon and Steven was famished by the time the last one left and he'd shown up at dusk on the cottage doorstep. He brought with him a bottle of wine, which Lindsay had anticipated, setting out two of her best crystal goblets on the sideboard.

While they sat on the bowlegged sofa together, sipping the wine and chatting, heavenly smells of her chicken dish filled the tiny house.

But Steven was dubious when she told him its name. "Green enchiladas?"

"Don't worry," she laughingly reassured him. "The green is for chili peppers."

When he had tasted the succulent chicken layered with tortillas, cheese and onions, and baked in a sauce of creamy chicken soup laced with chili powder and bright green pepper bits, he was immediately won over.

"Lord, this is good! But I have a feeling it's one of those dishes I won't be able to stop eating until I fall dead from gluttony."

Lindsay replied, "I hope it isn't so peppery it overpowers the bouquet of the wine."

He sipped. "It does. Just a little. But this time it doesn't matter." His wide smile turned devilish. "It isn't a Strake Farm wine, you see." And he helped himself to more chicken.

Lindsay couldn't remember a more pleasant evening. When the meal was over, Steven took part in clearing up and setting the kitchen to rights. To show her, he said with an air of masculine superiority, that he was capable of being as tidy as a woman any day of the week. Then he went off to the parlor with his coffee, leaving the cabinet doors wide open and his towel in a wet heap just as he had at home.

They talked for an hour as comfortably as if they had known each other for years. Then

Steven began to yawn. At a quarter of nine he laid a light kiss on Lindsay's forehead and took himself off to the clapboard farmhouse, calling back across his shoulder as he strode off through the moonlight that if there were any green enchiladas left over, he might be back for breakfast.

Putting out the light and locking the door, Lindsay reflected on the hours they had spent together. No sexual overtures. Her heart bumped a little at that. She found Steven disturbingly attractive, and she was relieved that in spite of his first bold overture, they had been able to enjoy each other the next evening simply as friends. After all, she had come back to Connecticut to straighten out her life. Not to further complicate it.

But when she was in bed, sleep eluded her. She kept remembering Steven's chaste kiss on her forehead, and staring out through the window at a canopy of stars, she tried to imagine what it would be like to nestle unreservedly in his arms.

Climbing out of bed, she padded over to the window and knelt in the chilly night air. At the top of the hill a light shone from an upstairs corner of her grandfather's house. Steven's house.

A pulse throbbed at the base of her throat. Steven was in the room where so many summer nights she herself had lain, thin cotton gowns veiling her nakedness while girlish yearnings she only vaguely understood churned in her loins.

But she wasn't a girl any longer. She stared at the square of light while an erotic vision sprang up in back of her eyes. Long, tanned torso arching above her ... golden flesh alabaster in the moonlight. ...

Shivering, she watched the light in the house on the hill go out, the image in her brain fading, though the stirrings of desire it had aroused remained achingly vivid. If Steven glanced out at the stars he was so fond of, would he look toward her cottage? Would he wonder if she was asleep?

What did Steven Strake think of her? Or did he think of her at all?

For the rest of the week, Lindsay wondered. Her uncertainty about the answer was the only unhappiness she experienced as the days passed. It nagged at her each time she saw Steven. When he passed through the labeling room, her skin tingled in anticipation of his arm brushing against hers or his hand laid lightly on her back while he paused to explain something. But usually all she was granted was a teasing whiff of his clean, woodsy smell or a maddeningly amiable greeting. He brought in a crate of grapes one day when she was operating the stemming machine, and she spent the next half hour trying to analyze his smile.

Her behavior was adolescent, she chided herself. It was ridiculous and demeaning. She liked him, she was attracted to him, but she wasn't really interested in him. Nor in any man. After what she had been through with Winston, she was quite content in her cottage with only her whimsical furniture to amuse her, so why was she agitating herself? What difference did it make what Steven Strake thought?

But still she couldn't shake off the desire to know.

ON FRIDAY afternoon Lindsay was on the terrace operating Lilliput by herself for the first time when Steven came out. She was nervous with him standing over her, but when she cut off the machine and turned around to face him, she felt his look of approval warming her like a ray of sunshine.

"You handled that like a professional."

She made a little bow, partly to hide the giddy feeling of happiness that swept over her. "Thank you, sir. I'm pleased to have pleased the boss."

"She's working okay now, is she?"

"Lilliput? Perfectly." Lindsay could understand his fondness for the bright yellow machine. It was fundamental to everything else that went on at the winery. The crushed, stemmed grapes went in, the juice came out. A quick, simple operation. If only the complications of life could be smoothed out so easily! She smiled up at him. "I wonder though, if the wine suffers without the human touch."

"Do you mean now that foot stomping is out of vogue?" Steven smiled too. "Actually there's a school of thought that supports that theory. Automation, they say, does too thorough a job of compressing the pulps and skins and gives a slight bitterness to the wine."

Lindsay's smoky eyes sparkled. "I'm learning so much! And it's all so fascinating. I never dreamed winemaking was such an art. I suppose like most people I've always taken for granted a fine bottle of Riesling or Chardonnay. But I certainly never will again."

Steven was silent looking down at her. Her dark hair was drawn back and tied at the crown with a pale blue ribbon. She wore a white shirt open at the throat and a pair of faded jeans that fit snugly over her sleekly curving hips. As her gaze locked with his, Lindsay quivered, certain he was about to take her in his arms. But it was an impression that in the next moment he dispelled with a casual comment.

"Rachel seems to think you'll be knowledgeable enough to help with the tours in a couple of weeks."

Feeling more deflated than she cared to admit, she forced a smile. "I hope so."

"You may not be so eager once you've had a taste of it."

"Maybe not. But I enjoy meeting people. If I'm able to answer their questions, I should think it might be fun."

Abruptly he changed the subject. "What are you doing later?"

"After work, you mean?" A stillness came over her. "I thought I might ask Katie to follow me to Hartford. I need to turn in my car at the rental agency." When he made no response, she added in a nervous rush, "I got rid of the U-Haul in Terrapin Falls earlier in the week."

"Katie probably has a date." He focused a direct gaze on her parted lips. "I'll drive over with you. We can have dinner afterward."

"Oh. Well, that's very nice. Yes. I'd like that."

"Six?" His eyes were still studying her mouth; two pinpoints of light in their dark centers challenging her with something undisclosed that made her throat tighten and her defenses come keenly alert.

"Six will be fine." She felt a surge of confidence and realized she was equal to his challenge, whatever it was. She had been wondering all week what he thought of her. She took a trembling breath. Perhaps tonight she might find out.

THE RESTAURANT Steven chose was called Annabelle's. They approached it from a small, dimly lit side street where Steven parked his car, a mellowed BMW that he told Lindsay he'd owned since Harvard.

He patted a fender as they got out. "The Old Gray Mare. That's what I call her when she's slow to start on a cold morning." Grinning, he tucked Lindsay's arm in his, drawing her close to his side as they headed toward the restaurant. "But I change her name to Stepping Sam when she's passing everything else on the turnpike."

"You have a grape press named Lilliput and a female BMW you call Stepping Sam." Lindsay shook her head as if in despair. "You're funny."

But her teasing tone reflected the ease she felt with him now. At the airport he had come to her rescue in a hassle over an obscure point in her car contract. Everyone in the rental agency had sat up and taken notice, and she was proud to be at his side. She was proud to be there now, too. Steven Strake was a handsome man and she liked the way he held her next to him as they walked . . . as if she were precious and fragile . . . as if he were looking forward as much as she was to a special evening. "Do you have names for all the inanimate objects that figure importantly in your life?"

With an air of gravity he answered, "I have a razor I call Jock whenever it nicks me. And an inseparable cup and saucer known among the crockery as Eleanor and Dr. White."

Her laughter produced a look of mock severity. "You're amused by that? Next time you're at my house, try mixing up my china and see what an uproar you create in the cupboard."

He stopped suddenly in a pocket of darkness cast by a maple and put his arms loosely around her shoulders. "Your turn to confess," he murmured. "What kinds of craziness are you guilty of?"

She gazed up into his eyes, luminous in the shadows. "I go out to dinner with lunatics."

She heard his low appreciative laughter, and then his mouth came down in what she anticipated would be a kiss as playful as their banter. But at once it turned into much more than that. The moment their lips met, a driving urgency sprang up between them. It seemed to Lindsay that a whole week of waiting went into the kiss. Her breasts flattened against his chest as his arms went around her. She leaned into his embrace, desire quickening along her spine. His hands slid down to her hips, molding her to his lower body, prolonging the moment they were locked together, heightening Lindsay's arousal in an alarming way. Shaken, she pulled back.

Her cheeks burned as she moved ahead of him into the pool of light before Annabelle's door. Struggling to regain her lightheartedness, she asked, "Have you mussed my hair?"

Steven's reply came back, "Not nearly so much as I'd like."

INSIDE THE RESTAURANT a slim woman in a sleek black dress greeted them, recognizing Steven and leading them across the candlelit dining room to a secluded table in an alcove. From another corner of the room came the thrum of a classical guitarist, while all around them muted voices mingled with the clink of fine crystal.

When they were seated, Lindsay, still recovering from his kiss, took a shaky breath. "Is this a favorite spot of yours? You're known here, it seems."

Steven's unreadable glance moved over her. "Annabelle knows me because she's one of the winery's best customers." He picked up the wine list from the table and pointed out the varieties offered that were Strake specialties.

Gradually Lindsay relaxed, listening to him. When he paused, she said, "I've been concentrating so hard all week on learning how our product is produced, I'd almost forgotten that in the outside world people are actually drinking it." Her gaze went out across the room again and in a moment she asked in a charged whisper, "Is that our Riesling?"

Steven's amused glance followed hers to a nearby table where the wine steward was tilting a familiarly labeled bottle. "It's a blend from season before last—our first year of actual production. Annabelle liked it so much she bought the whole yield."

His eyes returned to Lindsay. "I'm hoping that one we have in oak now will catch her fancy, too. Small wineries build their reputations mostly by word of mouth, and a lot of her customers are connoisseurs. We can use their business."

But Lindsay was still puzzling over something he had said at first. "In oak. What do you mean?"

"In oak barrels."

"Oh. Aging. I see." It seemed to her that Steven's attention was only half on what they were saying. Her own thoughts, too, were divided. A part of her was still outside, locked in his arms in the shadow of the maple. She moistened her lips. "How long is the wine left in the barrels?"

"Until the winemaker decides to take it out. I prefer more wood for some than for others, and those I leave longer. Three months, sometimes four. We'll be drawing this one off fairly soon, and then we'll see."

Lindsay watched his face grow more animated as they talked. When he fell silent, she said, "You love your work, don't you?"

"Winemaking? Yes." But he showed a reserve that surprised her. In a moment he added, "I love the law, too."

"Why did you give it up, then?"

"I haven't, really. I'm not practicing, but I'm still a member of the bar."

There was more to that, she felt, than his

answer revealed, but before she could think of how to draw him out further, the steward arrived with their own wine. Apparently Annabelle had anticipated Steven's choice, and when Lindsay tasted the delectably dry Macon Blanc that had been poured into her glass, her murmur of approval brought a faint smile to Steven's lips.

"When Strake Farm can turn out a vintage as perfect as this, I may hang up my hat and go back to Dexter, Brink and Dexter."

She wondered if he meant it and pursued the point. "Are you saying that winemaking is primarily a challenge? Is that its attraction?"

"One of them." He paused to order their meal—hickory-smoked trout with grated horseradish—and then he went on. "The life-style appeals to me as much as anything else."

"Then why didn't you practice law in a small town? Wouldn't that have done just as well?"

"A small town when corporate law is my passion?"

Warmth flooded Lindsay at his choice of words, but she pretended it was the effect of the Macon Blanc and not the memory of his kiss. "So you decided to compromise. You make a little wine, you read a little law."

His expression darkened. "I'm not a dilettante if that's what you're implying."

How swiftly his mood could change! "I wasn't implying that at all. Obviously you give your whole self to whatever you do. I only meant that you seem to have settled for the middle of the road. And apparently you're perfectly happy with your life just the way it is."

He eyed her silently for a moment and then abruptly changed the subject. "What kinds of songs do you write?"

His imperious air annoyed her. Tossing her hair back over one shoulder, she told him flatly, "Very good songs, according to my critics."

He laughed.

Her face flamed. "To quote you, it isn't bragging when one is telling the truth!"

She looked so agitated that he laughed again, but he took her hand in his and told her soothingly, "I'm sure you write wonderful songs."

"Then why are you making fun of me?"

"I'd never do that. I'm amused, that's all. Whenever you're feeling defensive you throw your hair around."

Her color heightened.

"As if you were a queen swishing her train."

There was so much boyish good humor glittering in his eyes that her pique gave way. "I know." The admission brought her lips down in a wry grimace. "I've always been teased about that haughty habit. If it would help to cut my hair, I would, but probably I'd just go on tossing my head anyway, the habit is so ingrained—and then I'd have to endure everyone's pity for having such a dreadful tic."

They laughed together at that and then Steven said quietly, "Don't cut your hair. It's too beautiful. And don't stop tossing your head either." His tone hoarsened. "Haughty or not, I like it."

Lindsay was grateful that this was the moment Annabelle came over to be introduced, and then the waiter chose to arrive with the food. The fresh brook trout was excellent and while they ate, Steven told entertaining stories of mishaps at the winery. But over dessert and coffee she thought wistfully of the remark he had made and wondered where it might have led if they hadn't been interrupted.

DRIVING BACK toward the farm, Lindsay found her thoughts straying again to the moments when Steven had held her in the darkness in front of Annabelle's. They seemed like a dream now.... During the evening Steven had observed her thoughtfully several times, his sensuous glance probing the soft white blouse that covered her breasts. They had danced, and she knew from the way he had fitted her body to his that he shared with her the excitement their closeness stimulated. But he made no reference to the way they had both ignited when their lips touched. In the car he kept his hands on the wheel.

However, when the BMW turned in at the farm, he took the road that led to the clapboard house instead of the winding trail that went down to the cottage.

Lindsay joked, but her heart was hammering. "Am I coming in for a nightcap?"

Shutting off the engine, he angled toward her in the seat, one hand resting lightly on the nape of her neck. "Come in for whatever you want."

His resonant murmur set her trembling, but she kept her voice steady. "I'd like a glass of sherry."

He gave her a long look before he opened the car door. "Sherry it is, then."

Following Steven into the house, Lindsay considered changing her mind. She was all too aware of how stimulated she was, of how even the touch of Steven's hand brushing hers as he reached for the gate latch set her quivering with arousal. She was stepping in too deep, too soon. She might regret this moment bitterly . . . and then it would be too late.

But when the light from the lamps in the parlor made warm circles on the burnished tabletops and the homespun curtains were drawn across the windows, she felt that in prolonging the evening she had done the only thing she could. Watching Steven start a fire in the stone fireplace, she admitted that, like the brittle kindling that blazed up from his match, there was too much smoldering between them, ready to flame up, to imagine they could simply say good-night. Without knowing exactly how or when, she had opened her life to Steven Strake, and he had come in. Now he was a part of all that concerned her, whether she liked it or not.

In a corner near the fireplace there was a piano she had noticed before, and now she asked Steven about it.

"It was my mother's," he told her. "No

one else had room for it, so it's mine now."

When he went out to the kitchen, she gave in to the pull it exerted on her and began to pick out a few notes that had haunted her for days.

At once the melancholy sweetness of the melodious sounds brought Steven to the door with the wine decanter in his hand. "What's the name of that?"

"It doesn't have a name yet." Glancing at him in the doorway, she realized with a shock how deeply committed she already was to him, to his broad sheltering shoulders and his steady blue gaze. Unnerved, she joked, "Perhaps I'll call it 'Dr. White's Song' and dedicate it to Eleanor."

But Steven was too intent to respond to her attempt at humor. He came and sat down on the bench beside her. "This is one of your songs? You're composing it now?"

His nearness intoxicated her, but she was put off by his amazement, as if he were discovering her, too, but not in a way she welcomed. "Does that seem so extraordinary?"

"Yes." This was the first time she had seen him the slightest bit ruffled. "I thought you wrote lyrics. Poems," he said in a way that told her he hadn't taken her work seriously. "But it's music you write." He stared at her. "What do you do? Do you pull the notes out of the air?"

"Really, Steven." Before her experience with

Winston, she might have appreciated so much flattering attention, but now she was sensitive to any misunderstanding of the talent that Winston had blamed for the breakup of their marriage. "I'm not the sword swallower at the circus, you know."

"Am I acting as if you're a freak?"

"A little, yes."

"I'm sorry." But he went on gazing at her, a frown creasing his heavy brow. "This is a new dimension of you that hadn't occurred to me. My fault altogether. I might have known that with a degree in music, you'd write the notes. It's English majors who write the lyrics, I suppose."

"I can write lyrics, too." Lindsay sighed. "Where's my sherry?"

He got up to get it, but when he came back he still wore the same preoccupied look. Setting her glass aside, he told her, "You can't have a drop of this until you finish playing the whole piece."

"That isn't possible at this point." But when she heard the sharpness in her tone, she added less abrasively, "I don't know how it ends."

He retreated to the couch then, urging her to go on, and for half an hour he listened quietly while the unfinished melody Lindsay fingered out on the keyboard drifted hauntingly through the house. At last she pushed back from the bench, bringing her glass of wine over to where Steven waited. She was bone weary all at once. There were times when composing exhilarated her, and other times like this when its elusiveness left her drained and frustrated.

"Why can't you finish it?" Steven challenged.

She fought the familiar, unreasoning irritation his question aroused. "I don't know why I can't." Winston had never understood either when she was deadlocked, particularly if it meant she would stick doggedly at the piano and cause a change in their plans. Perhaps Steven felt, as Winston had, that she was being deliberately temperamental.

But when she stood beside him, the smile that was so compelling creased his cheeks. Reaching out, he pulled her down next to him, fitting her into the curve of his arm so naturally that she melted against him, her irritation lessening as excitement began to build again.

"I like your music," he murmured near her ear. "But it's not for Eleanor and Dr. White. What you were playing is a *people's* love song."

She knew he was right. Even in its currently fragmented state, it couldn't be anything else. But love had been out of her life for so long ... she had forgotten how to follow where it wanted her to go ... forgotten ... or else she was afraid.

Her spine stiffened under Steven's caressing

fingers as she thought again of Winston and all the ways he had undermined her confidence in men. It definitely seemed a mistake now to have come in with Steven, to have let herself hope that beneath the strong pull of his sexual attractiveness she might have found a bedrock of caring.

She stirred in his arms, uneasy that in spite of everything, she was reluctant to leave him. "It's late, Steven."

"Is it?"

"We have to work in the morning." She started to pull away, but he blocked her with a series of softly persuasive kisses laid along her throat. An arm encircled her waist. The fingers that had played havoc with the nerves of her spinal column moved around and gently kneaded a breast.

"Don't go," he said huskily. "Stay with me tonight."

"Steven—" Her lips were dry, burning for his. "You don't know anything about me."

"You write music." His voice thickened, and inside she felt herself go soft with longing. "Your eyes are the color of autumn smoke." He reached around and turned off the lamp. Another one glowed dimly at the other end of the room and joined with the firelight in sending long shadows toward the dusky nest he made for her body at his side. "I know that your skin is the texture of peach petals and that once you lived at Christmas Church." His lips nibbled along the line of her earlobes. "What else is important?"

She had to be honest with him, she knew. Or else go back to the cottage. "I've been married, Steven."

She waited through one heartbeat and another before he said easily, hoarsely, "Have you?" But in the warm length of his body, which was curved around hers, she felt the jolt of her announcement.

"It matters, doesn't it, that I was married? That I'm not anymore."

"Does it matter to you?"

She said carefully, "I suppose it brands me as a certain kind of failure."

But he had stopped listening. His hands, skilled and provocative, opened her blouse and cradled her breasts in pliant, cupping palms. The tingling touch of his thumbs rubbing over her nipples sent another rush of arousal ripping through her.

She managed to gasp, "I don't want to make the same mistake again."

His hot whisper curled in her ear. "Haven't you learned, darling Lindsay? All our mistakes are brand new each time."

Then he kissed her mouth with a hunger she was powerless to resist. He kissed the scented softness below her ears—and hurrying, he kissed her closed, quivering eyelids and the

hollow of her throat where her pulse had gone
wild.

The need that had been growing in her all
evening spiraled out of control. The thought
occurred to her fleetingly that she might have
been a glacier in Winston's arms, but in Steven's she was a blazing bonfire. Twisting, she
flattened against him, feeling through to the
core of her the tightening of his muscles and
his flesh hardening to receive her.

Swiftly, deftly, he loosened her clothing.
Her slip slid away to the floor. The sweet
scent of her perfumed body rose between
them. Moaning, he buried his head against
her breasts, closing his lips on their erect
peaks, sliding his hands possessively over her
skin, peach-petal smooth and sensitive now
almost to frenzy.

Taut with restraint, Steven shed his own
clothes and swung her into his arms. On a rug
in front of the fire, he knelt above her.

Time halted. Then in a rapturous burst of
unleashed passion, Lindsay lifted to meet him.
A primitive wildness bounded through her. In
the darkness outside, a sleek-sided doe sprang
out across a dew-drenched clearing. The scent
of musk filled Lindsay's nostrils.

*Steven . . . he was all she had imagined he would
be . . . and so much, much more. . . .*

Glorying in the heavy, rasping breaths she
aroused, Lindsay clung to him, directing all

her energies toward matching his movements, toward injecting her own wiles into the lovemaking. But Steven was king, possessing the power that turned flesh upon flesh into precious agony, that brought them finally bursting out into the blazing light of sexual sensations more exquisite than anything Lindsay had ever known.

Afterward they lay still, Steven half covering her, cradling her in a tender, spent embrace that in its own way was as erotic as the tumult that had preceded it. Lindsay's thoughts drifted drowsily, her fingers entwined with his, their damp thighs touching.

Finally Steven roused. He kissed the curling tendrils of hair that framed her forehead and then he turned over on his side, claiming her still with one leg across the lower part of her body, but free now, up on his elbow, to look at the white loveliness of her with the firelight dancing on her breasts.

"Lindsay," he began.

But she stopped him with a fingertip laid gently on his lips. "Yes. You need to know about Winston, don't you?"

Steven's voice roughened. "Was that his name?"

"Winston West."

"Why aren't you Lindsay West?"

"Because I took my name back." She turned her head away. "I don't want anything in my life that belongs to him."

The blue of Steven's eyes deepened. "Am I allowed to hate him?"

"I can't stop you. But he isn't worth your energy, believe me."

Steven crooked a finger beneath her chin and brought her gaze back to his. "Tell me whatever you like."

Lindsay closed her eyes, seeing it all again like the speeded-up reel of a tawdry film. "We met in our last year in college. He was wealthy and fun-loving and he seemed totally smitten with me." She breathed in deeply. "We were married for a year and a half. He had an affair and I left him."

An ember snapped on the hearth. A rising wind rattled a pane behind the homespun curtains. "Did Winston West leave scars?"

Lindsay opened her eyes to meet Steven's penetrating stare. "Yes. But I didn't know until tonight," she whispered, "that the pain was gone."

Steven leaned over and kissed her lips. He kissed to rosiness the standing peaks of her breasts. Then he brought her up beside him, smoothing her satin skin, smoothing her long, dark hair back over her shoulders. In a voice tinged with regret he told her, "It does make a difference that you've been married. I do mind."

Lindsay went numb, hope shriveling inside her like a punctured balloon. So he wasn't the man she'd thought he might be. Bitterness edged her reply. "It's too bad you're disappointed, too bad I couldn't have come to you all starry-eyed and innocent."

A harsh sound of denial sprang from his throat, and he wrapped her quickly in his arms. "That's not what I care about." His urgent words sent new hope flaring in her brain like a scarlet banner. "What matters to me is that another man holds a place in your life. I despise that. I despise his claim on you. I want you all to myself, Lindsay Hancock. I don't want to share you with anyone, not even a memory."

A jubiliant cry rose in her throat. "Oh, Steven," she choked out. "Winston is only a darkness that once passed over the sun." She clung to him, welcoming the tidal wave of passion that swept over her, not caring any longer how vulnerable she was making herself or that emotionally she was at the mercy of a man others would say she hardly knew.

All she was conscious of as Steven brought her down again to the rug was the leashed power of his strong supple body hovering over her and the overwhelming tenderness with which he gathered her to him.

They lay together, and with eyes and lips, Steven praised every inch of her. Velvet-tipped fingers caressed the moist sheen of her breasts, the curves of her hips, the soles of her feet. Without haste he kissed and cajoled the secret centers of her desire until she was panting with urgency, and still he made her wait, dropping close-spaced kisses down her spine, settling half a dozen more in a circle on her nape. "Lindsay...." And then with startling swiftness he took her.

Lying in the flickering firelight afterward, Lindsay knew that no man but Steven Strake had ever made love to her.

5

STEVEN WOKE before dawn to the muted sounds of piano notes coming through the closed door of the bedroom. The space beside him where Lindsay had lain was vacant, the sheet cool to his touch. Climbing out of bed, he pulled a robe over his bare torso and went down the stairs.

The curtains were still drawn in the living room. A lamp burned beside the piano, and Lindsay—a wool afghan thrown across her shoulders—sat hunched on the bench, her forehead resting on the heel of one hand while the fingers of the other picked out again and again the same six notes.

Steven moved quietly to her side. "You're an early bird."

Lindsay swiveled her head around and gave him a quick smile, but her fingers went on with their work. "I'm sorry I woke you."

"How long have you been up?" He reached out and curved a possessive hand around the nape of her neck.

She shrugged and answered absently, "Not long. Oh, this damned B flat! It belongs in here somewhere, but not in this passage. And I can't get it out."

"Maybe later you'll be able to. After breakfast."

"No, I can't stop now." She flashed an apologetic look across her shoulder. "You go ahead. Don't wait for me."

"Lindsay, it's not even six o'clock." His hand stroked her shoulder and squeezed the soft flesh of her upper arm. "Let it go," he murmured. "Come back to bed for a while."

"I can't do that," she answered irritably. "I'm sorry. I don't mean to be cross. But I'm at such a critical point, Steven. I've got the whole thing running around inside my head. It's simply beautiful, but I can't get it out until I find where this flat belongs."

"I see." He took his hand away and jammed it into the pocket of his robe. "Then you'd rather I left you alone."

"Oh, yes, please. If you don't mind. I may get it in fifteen minutes, or it may take an hour." She laid restraining fingers lightly on his arm, her tone apologetic again. "I hope you can go back to sleep. This is terribly inconsiderate of me, I know. But if I don't catch the melody now, it may be gone forever."

"I understand." But nothing in the stiff manner in which he turned away indicated that he did. She watched him climbing the stairs and felt chilled suddenly—and panic-

stricken. That could be Winston closing the
door to the bedroom with angry finality. Except that it was Steven whom she had upset
this time, Steven in whose arms last night she
had found such utter joy . . . such release and
fulfillment.

Her gaze went back to the ivory keys her
fingers had automatically returned to. The
ability to compose was supposed to be a gift,
she thought bitterly, but at times like this, it
seemed more of a curse.

Yet in minutes she was lost again to her sur-
roundings. The melody Steven's lovemaking
had released demanded to be set free. The re-
calcitrant B flat at last fell into place. The music
began to pour forth through her fingers. Hast-
ily she rushed into the kitchen for the first
piece of paper that came to hand and a stub of
pencil to scratch down the notes.

An hour and a half later when Steven came
down again, shaved and dressed, she was still
hard at work. When she heard him clattering
around in the kitchen, she called out a greeting. He came to the doorway and answered
gruffly, but when she gave him only a vague
smile in return, he went back to his coffee-
making. At eight he shut the back door with
extra firmness. Lindsay was not even aware
that he had left.

IT WAS after ten o'clock when Lindsay surfaced
again. The brown grocery sack she had grabbed

in the kitchen was covered with squiggly bars and half notes, but she had her song. She got up from the piano, stretching, and filled with an incredible feeling of lightness and joy. The piece of music she held in her hand was the best thing she had ever written. It had freshness and depth and just enough sweetness. It was like a wonderful wine! She hugged the paper to her and swooped in a circle around the living room floor. Wait until she played it for Steven!

Then she saw the morning sun filtering through the homespun curtains, and her gaze flew to the clock on the mantel. Good grief! It was the middle of the morning! She was supposed to have been on the south slope picking grapes at eight o'clock. And Steven? She clapped her hands to her cheeks. He had left without a word. He must have been furious then. Imagine what he was now!

She took the stairs two at a time and threw on her clothes. Then she raced down the hill to her cottage, sick with apprehension that someone might see her still in the outfit she had worn to Annabelle's. But everyone was occupied on the far side of the barn, and she managed to get into her jeans and dash back before she met Katie, bent over the water cooler on the terrace.

"A diller, a dollar," the freckle-faced girl sang out when she saw her. "The ten o'clock scholar arrives at last."

Lindsay flushed to the roots of her hair. "Am I fired?"

"Well—" Katie raised shoulders and eyebrows. "The boss isn't in a very good mood. In fact, he isn't speaking to anyone." Then she burst out laughing. "But he'll get over it if you have a good excuse."

With palpitating heart, Lindsay followed her down the path, toward the rows of Johannesburg Rieslings gleaming translucently in their heavy green clusters. Everyone was on hand... Rachel with a bonnet covering her curly gray locks, her husband Tom, Clint Phelps, and Clint's young wife.

Katie whispered, "The transient pickers didn't show up. We may have to call out the volunteer fire department before we get through."

Lindsay groaned, "Of all days for me to be late!"

Steven was picking at the end of the last row. He looked up when she and Katie appeared, but he gave no sign of acknowledgment. As soon as Lindsay could manage it, she worked her way toward him.

Abreast of him at last, she said in a breathless rush, too low-pitched for the others to hear, "Would you like to have my head on a silver platter?"

He raised his cool blue eyes. "I'd rather have help in the field when I need it."

"I'm terribly sorry. I know that an apology

doesn't mean much when you're shorthanded." She began snipping furiously with her pruning shears. "Or when your houseguest is selfish enough to wake you up before six o'clock in the morning and then doesn't even fix your breakfast."

Unexpectedly, the warmth came back into his voice. "What I missed more was a goodbye kiss."

She glanced up quickly.

"You didn't even hear me leave, did you?"

"Oh, Steven, that's the way I am. When I'm composing, everything else fades out of focus."

His wonderful grin creased his cheeks, and she felt relief spreading through her like a blessed elixir. He said, "That's really what I was annoyed about, you know. I told you last night that I didn't want to share you with anyone, not even a memory." His blue-eyed gaze traveled over her. "Music falls into that category, too."

Lindsay stiffened. In a voice that was discordant even to her own ears, she said, "Then last night was a terrible mistake."

Steven's brows jumped together. "Cut it out, Lindsay. I'm joking."

"You picked the wrong subject." She moved down the opposite side of the row, her edged tone slicing the air between them. "Music is serious business with me. It's my top priority. I don't kid around about it."

His strong chin jutted. "You kidded around about it the first day we met."

"You were a stranger then."

"I'm not a stranger now? I feel like one. I held you in my arms last night, but now I feel like you've slammed the door in my face and thrown away the key."

Her gaze locked with his. She realized numbly this wasn't Winston she was talking to, and her icy reserve shattered. "Oh, forgive me, Steven." She swallowed back the surprising rush of tears that crowded her throat. "I'm doing all the wrong things, saying all the wrong things. And the day started out so wonderfully, too."

The row turned, and they moved out of sight of the others before she spoke again. "The song I began last night and finished after you left is the first really good piece of work I've done since I left college."

"What about California?" he said.

She hesitated, following with her eyes the glint of his shears in the sunlight. "I was competent in California, good enough that they begged me to stay. But everything I wrote there was automated, high tech, plastic."

He glanced up at her, his shears stilled. "And the song you wrote this morning?"

She gave him a clear-eyed gaze. "Straight from the heart."

"I'm glad."

"The thanks go to you."

"Why?"

Her voice throbbed softly, "I thought the music in me was dead. But it was only sleeping. You woke it up."

He grinned. "Then we're even. It woke me up." But in his bottomless blue eyes she could find no laughter, and a chill swept over her. He must still resent the way she had behaved this morning. He must feel that it was her passion to compose that had closed the door in his face.

She bent and lifted the half-filled basket of clustered grapes she had picked. "You take this," she told him. "Yours is full. I'll go and empty it."

WITHIN TWO DAYS all the Rieslings were harvested, crushed, and the juice fermenting in the vats; but the work on the other vines and inside the winery went on at a furious pace until the end of another week. Contrary to normal expectations, the Chardonnays had outproduced the other grapes and demanded immediate attention. The yield was especially heavy on the vines to the west of the Rieslings, a circumstance Steven attributed to the climactic difference between one part of the vineyard and the other.

"You've got to be kidding!" Lindsay laughed when she heard him make that statement. "The whole vineyard covers only twenty-five acres."

But the other members of the team upheld him. They were sitting in the living room at Steven's house on Saturday night, celebrating the end of a rough two weeks with a toasting party.

Shy Clint said expansively, "Every viticulturist knows there are climactic variations in even the smallest vineyard." And then they all laughed at the flaming color that rushed to his cheeks.

Steven said, "You've learned quite a lot tinkering with the machinery, haven't you, Clint boy?"

"But he's right, nevertheless," Rachel came to Clint's defense. "It stands to reason, too, don't you think? On a cold day the brow of the hill takes a lot more wind than the valley a few hundred yards away."

"And the nine inches of rain we had in two days last spring stood around in the valley a lot longer than it did on the hill," Katie put in.

Laughing, Lindsay said, "I stand corrected." She lifted her wineglass. "Here's to the cold toes and the warm shoulders of our vineyard. Or vice versa."

In unison they sipped from the '78 Marechal Foch that Steven had generously provided, and then Steven raised his glass with another toast. "Here's to this year's crush. May it be the finest one so far."

Watching him over the rim of her goblet, Lindsay thought back over the time she had been on the farm. In so many ways she had already begun to heal. Coming back to Connecticut had been a good idea after all. It was balm to her soul to discover that the roots she had put down as a child were still vibrantly alive in the heavy silt loam of her grandfather's farm. But despite her high spirits this evening, a good many other evenings preceding this one had been long and lonely. Twice she had asked Steven to come to dinner, but both times he had begged off to do book work. At twilight on another evening she had been about to climb the hill to his house when she saw him drive off in the Old Gray Mare. She had spent that night roaming restlessly around her cottage until she had heard the car's wheels grinding on the gravel driveway at a quarter after eleven.

The song she had written had set loose in her brain half a dozen other tunes, and she did what she could with them in her house alone, but she lacked a piano, and her pride wouldn't allow her to ask Steven if she might use his.

But glancing again at his relaxed face, Lindsay reflected that probably things had worked out for the best after all. She felt a hollowness every time she thought of the rapture she had experienced in Steven's arms the night after their dinner at Annabelle's. But those erotic moments were balanced by the unrest he had stirred up in her the next morning. She had vowed after her divorce never again to allow anyone to curtail her freedom to compose. Being Winston's wife had taught her a bitter lesson about the damage that could occur when one person's will imposed itself on the lifeblood of another. She would be better off alone for the rest of her life than to put herself through that again.

But tonight she was part of a big happy family, each of them proud of the hard hours they had put in, and now enjoying their leisure together.

"Shall I get some more cheese?" Lindsay asked Steven when Tom Byrd speared the last crumb from the plate she had arranged earlier and brought over from her own cottage. "There's more of your Brie in the kitchen, isn't there?"

"I'll come with you and see." But when they were alone in the kitchen, he laid his hands on her shoulders and turned her around to face him. He startled her by saying huskily, "I've missed you, Lindsay."

"How can that be?" Her heart was hammering, but she hung on to the casual air that had seen her through hours of working at his side without a single affectionate glance. "We haven't missed a day seeing each other."

"You know what I mean."

She brought her chin up and tossed her hair. "I'm afraid I don't. You'll have to tell me."

He took the cheese tray from her and set it

on the drainboard. "I'd rather show you." His mouth came down on hers, and at once a familiar prickling spread from her spine to her loins. She thought angrily, he had an uncanny ability to arouse her.

She pulled back. In response to his frown, she said, "You've hardly spoken to me in the past two weeks. Do you expect me to melt in your arms?"

"I don't expect you to." His gaze burned into her. "I thought you'd want to."

"Kisses doled out sparingly are that much more eagerly sought after. Is that your theory?"

His arms tightened around her. "Don't be cynical, Lindsay. It makes you seem hard and unapproachable, and you aren't."

A bitter laugh escaped her. "It's easy to see why you'd think that."

His gaze leveled. "Because we were so quick to make love? And to do it so satisfactorily?"

She felt her face grow hot.

"That's why I've stayed away. You came back here to get your bearings. I decided you needed time alone to do that without any pressure from me." He brought his mouth close to hers again. "But two weeks is long enough, don't you think?"

She trembled. "I thought you were angry."

He kissed her lips lightly half a dozen times as if they held a sweetness he couldn't get enough of. "For a couple of hours that Saturday morning I was angry. I wanted you to come back to bed with me. It was humiliating playing second fiddle to a piano."

"It wasn't a question of that."

He chuckled dryly. "I realized that when I was picking grapes. The piano had the whole field to itself. I wasn't even in the running, was I?"

She wriggled to free herself from his embrace, but he held on to her tightly, kissing her between his words. "Don't fight me, Lindsay. Don't fight what we've found."

"I'm not ready for anything serious."

"Except your music." He let her go then and stood back from her with his arms folded across his chest. "Never mind that last crack. Forget it. Let's start over."

She picked up the tray again and said primly, "We came out here to get some cheese."

"Maybe you did," he said huskily. "What I came for was a kiss—and to ask you to stay after the others leave." He spoke again quickly before she could say no. "I haven't heard your song."

She turned around from the refrigerator, her smoky eyes full of distrust. "You don't really want to, do you?"

"Are you saying I'm using that as bait?"

"Are you?"

"I'm not above that. If there's no other way to keep you here." The glint in his eyes sent a shiver of desire dancing up her backbone. He had left the scent of his after-shave on her skin and every nerve in her body was responding to it.

She raised her chin defiantly. "I think I'll go out and play it now. Then everyone can hear it."

His eyes darkened. "If that's what you want," he came back at her evenly, "then by all means do."

THE GATHERING in the parlor did move to the piano. Lindsay played, and Katie's strong, clear soprano carried them through an assortment of old favorites. There were ample pauses in between for Lindsay to introduce her own composition, but recalling Steven's cool gaze in the kitchen, she let the others choose the songs.

The clock struck eleven and one by one the others began to say good night. Lindsay got very busy carrying glasses out to the kitchen. She had her hands in soapy water when the front door closed for the last time. In the parlor, she heard Steven picking out on the piano the refrain of the last song they had sung, and then she heard his footsteps coming toward the kitchen.

When she turned around after a minute, he was standing in the doorway watching her dry her hands on her apron.

Her eyes flicked away from his solid gaze. "That was a fun party."

"You don't have to clean up."

"I know. I don't mind." She dried her hands more thoroughly than she needed to. "I'm sorry I acted like a cat a while ago." She made herself look at him again. "The truth is I've been waiting for days for the right moment to play my song for you. When we could be alone," she murmured. "You inspired it. I wanted you to hear it before anyone else."

He was quiet so long she had to bite her tongue to keep from adding something stupid and nonsensical just to break the silence. Then he came to her and gathered her into his arms. But instead of the kiss she expected, he held her close, his cheek resting on the top of her head.

He said hoarsely, "We've been alone all evening, didn't you know? When you're in a room, you light it up. Nobody else is visible."

Her throat tightened. "Oh, Steven—"

"It was a hell of a long two weeks without you." Then he took her face gently between his hands and kissed her.

6

WITH STEVEN'S short bathrobe wrapped twice around her, Lindsay got up early on Sunday morning—not to go to the piano this time, but to fix a sumptuous breakfast for Steven. She had the pancake batter mixed, the coffee on and the bacon in the pan when its tantalizing aroma finally lured him down the stairs.

She lifted a welcoming face to his kiss. Last night she had discovered anew his passion and his tenderness when they made love before the embers in the fireplace. Afterward his reaction to her song was to ask her to play it several more times. And then he danced with her in the firelight, humming every note perfectly as they moved slowly and sinuously to its haunting melody.

In the sunlight of the kitchen, she said against his furry chest, "I was about to set the table."

He nuzzled her soft neck. "I like the flowers."

A cluster of yellow daisies with dew still on them were arranged in a white cream pitcher in the center of the cloth she had found in one of the drawers. "They're growing by the back door. Had you noticed?"

He ambled away. "I've noticed a glaring oversight on my part. I've forgotten to introduce you to two very important personages."

"Steven! I'm not presentable."

"You'll do. Close your eyes." Instead of going out the door to fetch whoever was going to embarrass her mightily, he began rummaging around among the dishes. After a minute he said in the voice of a carnival barker, "One for the money, two for the show. Now you can look."

She opened her eyes and in his outstretched hand she saw a thick, white saucer.

"Dr. White," he said with a flourish. "And Eleanor."

The cup he brought from behind his back was a small, flowered demitasse, a striking contrast to the dime-store crockery in his other hand.

But it wasn't the incongruous match that startled Lindsay. "Steven!" she cried out. "That's my grandmother's Haviland!"

A smile creased his craggy face. "Ah, Eleanor. At last you have a family. I always knew you were from good stock."

Lindsay crowded into the narrow space where he stood. "But where on earth? How?" She reached to take hold of the fragile piece of china she had loved so as a girl.

"The answer to *where*," said Steven, "is the farthest corner of the middle shelf. The *how* came about last summer when I painted the insides of the cabinets."

Lindsay moaned, "Once there were six in this set."

"Sorry, but Eleanor alone survives. Apparently all the rest have gone on to porcelain heaven. Which probably explains why she got left behind. But fortunately," he intoned, "frail Eleanor has found true love and lasting happiness with H. Woolworth White as her support."

Giggling, Lindsay asked, "What does the H stand for?"

"It's the conglomerate initial for the Housewares and Kitchen Utensils, center aisle, ma'am, two rows back."

"You nut!" Lindsay laughed, and stood on tiptoes to wrap her arms around his neck. "Whatever made you match them up?"

He set the cup and saucer aside and circled her waist with his hands. "The union was complete before we met. Whoever cleaned out the house after your grandparents died must have had short arms. Hopkins, who came afterward, was a salty old bachelor who took all his meals with Rachel's mother-in-law. I doubt if he ever even came into the kitchen. When I decided to paint, I shone a flashlight into the hinterlands, and there were Eleanor and H. Woolworth back in a corner, all snuggled up. It would have been a crime to part them."

Lindsay raised softened lips and murmured, "What a funny lawyer you are."

"I'm a winemaker. Winemakers have license to do all sorts of crazy things."

"You're not fooling me. In your heart of hearts you're a lawyer. When I got out of bed this morning, I stumped my toe on Volume Two of Franklin Shares Incorporated vs. the State of Rhode Island."

"Cook, look to the stove," Steven rebuked mildly. "The bacon is burning."

LATER, FINISHING up breakfast, Lindsay poured coffee into "frail Eleanor" and said to Steven, "I think it's terribly romantic that I'm sitting here in this kitchen with you, drinking coffee from my grandmother's long lost Haviland." *And that we've fallen in love,* she wanted to add. But it was too soon to say that. That would be tempting fate when their feelings for each other were still new, untried in so many ways. Besides, she wasn't at all sure that she wanted to be in love.

However, gazing across the table at the face that in such a short time had become so dear to her, she acknowledged that her will had played a very small part in what was happening to her heart. She had wanted her feet to be firmly planted on solid ground before she even thought about a man in her life again. But her feelings for Steven had simply exploded inside her. This was crazy business, she reflected, sitting at the table with both of them wearing Steven's robes when less than twenty-four hours ago she had made up her mind that she was better off alone, living her life the way she wanted to without any interference from anyone.

But she was too happy to analyze the situation. All she wanted was to bask in the warm sunshine that was streaming across the table and to contemplate the day ahead.

Steven had suggested a picnic. There was a woods joining the vineyard that had a stream and massive granite boulders where they could spread everything out.

"We can even take a nap," he had said, his heavy-lidded gaze suggesting that he might have something else in mind.

Lindsay smiled to herself and pushed back her chair. "A picnic sounds romantic, too," she told Steven as she gathered up some of the dishes and carried them to the sink. "But are you sure they can spare us at the winery? On a day like this, there are bound to be dozens of people out for drives in the country. The tours will be packed."

Steven rose and stretched his lanky body. "That's all the more reason for us to stay out of the way. Clint and Rachel can handle it."

"I'm sorry for Dorothy." Lindsay thought of

Clint's young bride. "She'll be lonely on such a lovely day."

Steven came up behind her and crossed his arms over her breast. "Do you want to ask her to go with us?"

"No, thank you, sir. But you could at least call her up and tell her she's welcome at the winery. She could pour the wine for the tasting or something."

"I told her last night." Steven nibbled one of Lindsay's earlobes. "You see? I think of everything."

She turned around in his arms and leaned against him with a sigh of contentment. "You do. You're a very nice man, do you know that?"

"Prove you mean it by fixing us a super lunch, will you?" His words seemed a kind of dismissal, but he delivered them in a husky murmur that told her otherwise. They stood for a long time at the sink in the sunshine, kissing, while Lindsay's hands, holding the memory of his body, delighted her with all the ways she was free to touch him . . . and to be touched in return.

IN THE WOODS where Lindsay and Steven stopped for their picnic, Lindsay could hear car doors slamming as tourists arrived at the winery, and once, the sound of Rachel's clear throaty laughter came floating through the air. But a thick growth of wild cherry trees and mountain laurel bunched between towering elms and hemlocks made their pastoral retreat seem miles from civilization.

"Oh, this is heavenly," Lindsay breathed, gazing up at a patch of blue sky that domed the clearing.

Steven set down the picnic basket and settled comfortably on the boulder beside her. "You should see it in the spring after the snow melts."

"I remember." She closed her eyes. "Hepatica first and then yellow dogtooth violets."

"Followed at once by jack-in-the-pulpits and cowslips growing along the swamp pools."

Lindsay turned to regard him lazily. "Which season do you prefer? Spring, when everything is tender and green? Or now, when all of nature is teetering on the brink of winter?"

"I like every season for its own special charms." His blue eyes drifted slowly over her. "But it seems to me this particular fall has more to say for itself than usual."

Still basking in the glow from their earlier lovemaking, she teased him a little with a fingertip, tracing the shape of his mouth. "I like winter best. That's what I missed in California—the hushed silence an evening holds when it's snowing . . . soup bubbling on the stove . . . a crackling fire—"

"We had a fire last night," he said huskily. He took a long taste of the honeyed sweetness of her mouth and then pulled her close.

Lindsay whispered against his shoulder, "Last night was wonderful, Steven."

"You were wonderful." His fingers traveled lingeringly along her throat. "Do you know what I thought when I woke up and found you gone?"

"Tell me."

"That I'd dreamed you." He dipped his hand inside the collar of her shirt and stroked the rounded fullness of her breast. "I lay there thinking that everything was over." He paused. "And then I smelled bacon."

Lindsay pushed him away, laughing. "You're so romantic!"

"Only on picnics." Lifting the lid of the hamper, he peered inside. "Tell me what you've tucked away in here."

"Never mind. It's too early to think of eating again. You're full of bacon, remember?" Still tingling from his touch, she breathed deeply and glanced around. "I think this must be the same clearing where I used to come and hunt for gold."

"Gold." Steven leaned back, laughing. "You'd be more likely to find nickel here if you found anything."

"Leprachaun's gold," Lindsay said with mock disdain.

"Are you Irish?"

"I don't have to be to have read Irish fairy tales and become enthralled by them."

"I'll bet you never found any of the gold you read about."

"The next thing to it—pennies," she answered, with a distant expression. "It was years before I caught on to the fact that my grandfather was hiding them for me."

Steven's glance was gently speculative. "You had a happy childhood, didn't you?"

Lindsay met the tenderness in his blue eyes. "Happier than I realized at the time. I was always thinking about tomorrow."

He said softly, "And then tomorrow came and it wasn't what you'd dreamed it would be."

Lindsay sighed. "I thought when I married Winston that I'd entered a sort of guaranteed state of automatic fulfillment. It's hard to imagine now that I could have been so innocent. Or so mistaken about a man."

"That's all in the past, Lindsay."

"The past has a way of infecting the future."

"Only if you allow it to."

"I've found that bits and pieces sometimes pop up of their own free will."

Steven gazed at her steadily. "Then the thing to do is to put them in their proper perspective. Don't give them more weight than they're worth."

A smile turned up her lips. "Have you always been so wise?"

"Far from it." He chuckled. "Don't you

know that it's easier to tell someone else how to solve his problems than it is to solve your own?"

"Then it's my turn, isn't it?" She folded her hands primly. "Tell me your problems, Mr. Strake."

He regarded her solemnly. "I have two, madam. Whether to kiss you now ... or whether to wait another five minutes."

Her look softened. "I have the answer." Lacing her arms around his neck, she put her lips to his. "Now."

THE SUN HAD SHIFTED far to the west before Steven and Lindsay got back to considering their lunch.

While Steven uncorked a bottle of wine, Lindsay pulled foil-wrapped packets from the hamper. "Carrot sticks, ham sandwiches, dill pickles and cheese straws."

Steven lifted his brows in amazement. "Where on earth did you find cheese straws?"

"One doesn't find them," Lindsay said reprovingly. "One concocts them with infinite care and patience and then tucks them away in the freezer for that special occasion when ordinary chips simply will not do."

"Such foresight," Steven clucked. But the crisp cheese straws she unwrapped met with his instant approval. "More," he commanded, and opened his mouth like a starving bird.

Lindsay fed him one, and then another.

"That isn't more," he objected while he turned his attention back to the wine. "That's rationing."

"Then help yourself." Lindsay took the cup of wine he had poured for her. "We offered every toast last night that I can think of. Shall we just sip this and be grateful for a gorgeous day?"

Lifting his own cup, Steven focused on her lips, parted in a questioning smile. "That's toast enough, isn't it—a gorgeous day, a marvelous wine—" his voice stretched out huskily "—and the most beautiful woman in the world."

Lindsay's cheeks colored prettily. "Only in the state of Connecticut. And if you keep giving me looks like that, this will turn out to be the first seven-course picnic in history."

He taunted lightly, "With more than finger bowls in between, eh?"

Lindsay's smoky eyes laughed at him. "You're insatiable."

"It's all your fault. You shouldn't kiss me as if I were the last man on earth."

Lindsay's lips formed a surprised oval. "Do I do that?"

Steven munched his sandwich smugly. "It's a terrific aphrodisiac."

"You're embarrassing me!"

"Am I? I don't know why. It's certainly

nothing to be ashamed of to be able to make a man feel he's everything a woman could desire."

Lindsay's cheeks turned crimson. "You make it sound as though it's a skill I've deliberately practiced."

He shot her a sidelong glance that was meant to be as wicked as his blue eyes made it. "You can deliberately practice with me as often as you like."

"Steven—I mean it!" Her color deepened. "You're making me feel cheap!"

Reaching out with the rough masculine firmness with which he sometimes masked his tenderness, he told her, "Don't be angry." His nibbling kiss moved along her cheekbone while he held her wrists captive against his chest. "I'm teasing about everything ... everything except the way you make me feel, which is too wonderful, too special ever to tease about." He drew back to look into her eyes. "Don't you think I know how spontaneous, how fresh and vibrant your lovemaking is?"

Her chin quivered. "I don't know. I'm not sure now about anything."

"You can be sure about this." He kissed her swiftly, his tongue and lips hard on hers, claiming her more certainly than ever before. Releasing her, he went on, "You can be sure I know when you come to me, that you come with your whole heart, with a purity of feeling I could never doubt, with a singleness of mind that could never be cheap." He grasped her shoulders and pulled her close again. "You can be sure I know how lucky I am, because you are very, very special, Lindsay Hancock."

She stayed in his arms for a few minutes, trusting again in the thud of his heart close to her own, in his breath hot against her cheek. Then she pulled away slowly. "Thank you, Steven."

He curved a finger under her chin and raised her eyes to meet his. "Thank you, my darling."

A peace settled over them after that, and they finished their lunch, able after a little while to enter again into the easy comfortable banter they had enjoyed at breakfast. At the close of the meal, Steven brought two chocolate bars out of his jacket pocket, and they sat on a hollow log at the edge of a brook to eat them.

Lindsay smiled across at Steven. "How sinfully delicious! I can't remember how long it's been since I've indulged in a whole candy bar at one sitting."

"That's odd." His lips turned up in sly amusement. "When you keep a drawerful of candy bars at the cottage."

Lindsay gasped. "How do you know that?"

He grinned roguishly. "I discovered your secret cache while I was drying the dishes the night of the green enchiladas. I thought it was the silver drawer." He clucked again with his tongue. "Chocolate crumbs every-where. I thought perhaps you might keep a pet mouse."

Lindsay sighed her chagrin and tucked in her already flat stomach. "I've always had a dreadful weakness for sweets. But I only allow myself tiny nibbles."

His gaze swept over the trim lines of her figure. "Obviously, my darling, you're not gorging yourself. You deserve a treat today." He tweaked her cheek. "It'll do you good to get this vice out in the open."

She pouted a little. "You sound as if you approve of vices."

"I do. In poetesses."

"What?"

"A poetess is what I thought you were that first day you showed up on the terrace announcing that you were a songwriter."

Lindsay flushed. "You didn't believe me?"

"I believed you wrote lyrics. I imagined you might be one of those 'moon-and-June rhymers' who float along with their feet off the ground. You can't guess how pleased I was to discover those chocolate crumbs. They assured me your size sixes were mired in clay the same as mine."

She eyed him saucily. "Are you also a secret chocolate eater, Steven?"

"In spurts," he confessed. "But my darkest secret is that I'm a poet scorner. Not of Whitman or Frost or anyone who seriously writes verse," he added at her look of dismay. "The ones I run from are those who try to palm off their doggerel as bona-fide sonnets." He fastened his eyes on Lindsay. "Which they sometimes put to music."

Lindsay said sternly, "So that's how you sized me up."

He grinned. "Not really. But I wasn't aware until you sat down at my mother's piano that you were a composer." His smile grew thoughtful. "It took me a while to adjust to that."

Lindsay's heartbeat accelerated. Why did her music always stand in the way when she least wanted it to? "Is that why you acted as if I were a trained bear?"

He squeezed her hand. "I was awed. I'd never met a composer before."

She asked carefully, "Did it make a difference?"

"Judging from what happened afterward," he murmured, "you ought to know it didn't. But I realized when I heard you playing your own composition that there was a complexity behind your beautiful face that I had been only vaguely aware of." He gazed solemnly at her. "I knew that sooner or later I'd have to deal with it."

Sooner or later. Which was this, she wondered. If it were the former, there could be years of lovely days ahead like this one. But if not, then this glorious autumn day might signal the winding down...she would go on working for a few months longer at the winery, and then she would move on, as he expected her to. . . .

Her pleasure in the bubbling brook and the clear sky dimmed. She asked in a voice not quite steady, "Have you solved your dilemma yet?"

"Have you solved yours?" he answered evenly.

"What do you mean?"

"When you came here, you told me your reason was to get your bearings." He paused. "Has that happened?"

Lindsay glanced away. "Not totally." She moistened her lips. "But I'm coming along nicely."

He slipped an arm around her. "Am I helping or hindering?"

"Helping, definitely." She nestled gratefully into his embrace, her spirits reviving. "I've never felt so content in my life."

"You don't hear New York calling?"

She lifted her eyes and searched the depths of his. "I do. But the call is faint and far away. I'm not nearly ready for that, Steven. I'm like a wobbly legged colt. Someday I hope to run in the Derby. But not yet."

"Good girl," he muttered huskily. He bent his head and kissed her. "Then I can keep you a little while longer."

Her response leaped to her lips. *You can keep*

me forever if you like! But she held it back. In less than a day they had come a long, long way. *Live in this moment,* her inner self warned, *and let tomorrow take care of itself.*

7

IT WAS NEARLY FIVE when Lindsay and Steven returned to the winery after their picnic. Lindsay would have enjoyed staying longer beside the bubbling little stream Steven had led her to. The woods were ablaze with color and the walk they took through them hadn't lasted nearly long enough. Flaming ivy garlanded every tree trunk. And witch hazel, covered with delicate yellow flowers, made spots of sunshine in all the hollows. But Steven announced that he had to get back before Rachel closed the winery.

For days he had been keeping close tabs on the contents of the tanks. The Rieslings were ready to come off, and the space was desperately needed. Today, he told her, might be the day he could begin draining the vats so they could be cleaned and filled again.

While he was downstairs running his tests, Lindsay lingered in the tasting room on the ground level of the barn, waiting for him to go home with her for supper. The area was crowded with the last tour of the day, and she stood over in a corner chatting with Dorothy until he was ready to leave.

Laughingly, she confided in Clint's pretty bride, "If Steven does decide to empty the vats, tomorrow will be a scary day for me."

"Why?" the girl inquired.

"Because Katie is scheduled to show me how to crawl inside of them and scrape the tartrates out."

Dorothy's china blue eyes widened. "I'd die if I had to do that!"

"I may, too." A shiver ran over Lindsay. "I'm not exactly looking forward to it."

Dorothy shot her a quizzical look. "Do you like working here?"

"Yes." Lindsay paused. One of her chief concerns at the first had been that she might not fit in. Steven had taken a big chance including her in his closely knit team. However, it seemed to her that everything had worked out nicely. She felt she was pulling her part of the load, but if Dorothy was wondering how she felt about her job, perhaps Clint and the others had been talking. "Why do you ask?"

Diffidently, Dorothy lifted a shoulder. "I don't know. It's just that you have a degree from a university, and you write songs, don't you? Katie said so. It just seems funny that you wouldn't rather do something more in your line than picking grapes and putting corks in bottles."

Lindsay had to smile. "People sometimes starve writing songs."

But when Dorothy turned away to answer a tourist's question, Lindsay regretted that she had hedged. She had made a very good living at the California studio writing background music for television. She could go back there and do the same thing today if she wanted to. She should have said so and then explained that she was enjoying a holiday at the winery.

But that would have sounded condescending, she realized. Besides, it wasn't true. She had been desperately in earnest when she came to the winery seeking work. It was only now, when her life was beginning to come back into focus, that she could forget for hours, for days even, the misery she had felt on the West Coast. The futility of her work. The sense of not belonging anywhere.

It was Steven who was responsible for her recovery. She glanced around the crowded room. Steven and this blessed place that was so full of sweet memories. Dorothy might think it was odd that she was here, but Lindsay knew that for now, for a while longer at least, this was where she belonged. Later. . . . Her heart skipped a beat. Later if things worked out as she had begun to dream this afternoon that they might, she and Steven might take an apartment in New York. He missed his law practice. She was sure of that. It was too soon to mention it, of course, but it had occurred to her that eventually Rachel might be persuaded to take on the management of the winery. Then she and Steven could work in the city and spend their weekends and vacations overseeing the vineyard. She was in the midst of picturing a loft they might rent in Soho—hanging curtains, actually, and watering pots of African violets on the windowsills—when a familiar voice at her elbow said her name.

"Lindsay Hancock? I don't believe it."

She whirled around to face a compact, dark-haired man who had stepped out of the crowd to smile at her. "Jonathon Page? I don't believe it, either! What are you doing here?"

His gaze traveled over her as he took her hands in his. "I'm touring the winery, what else?"

The last time Lindsay had seen Jonathon was when the two of them had teamed up as composer and lyricist to create the smash musical hit of their senior year at Boston U. Then she had married Winston, and Jonathon had gone off to Paris to work in the Folies. "Are you back in New York?"

"I've been back for a year and a half. Don't you read the papers? I wrote the lyrics for *Fireflies* and *Rain on the Roof*."

Lindsay knew both productions had enjoyed good runs off Broadway, but she had deliberately tuned out the details of the show talk she had heard in California. "I've been a little out of touch."

"So it seems." Her dark-haired friend steered her over toward the door where there was more breathing space. "What are you doing hiding out here in the country?"

"I'm not hiding." But with an unpleasant little shock she realized that Jonathon's description of her reluctance to take on a full-time musical career before she had her priorities straightened was fairly accurate . . . and the cowardice his tone implied was mildly justified at least. Less spiritedly she added, "I'm resting up from some time I spent doing television on the Coast."

Jonathon's piercing black eyes glittered knowingly. "It's a rat race out there, isn't it?"

She prickled defensively. Jonathon had always put her a little on edge, even though he was terribly talented and wonderful to work with. She tossed her hair back over her shoulder. "It was lucrative at any rate."

He went on staring at her, a sardonic little smile hovering on his lips. "But you got tired of making money and came up to Connecticut. To pick grapes, of all things.

Lindsay's mouth opened. "How do you know that?"

He nodded toward Dorothy, standing now with Clint. "I'm afraid I eavesdropped when you were talking to that girl."

Lindsay's color deepened as she recalled her

remark about starving. "Then you must have concluded, mistakenly, I assure you, that I didn't make out too well in California."

He answered shrewdly, "What I concluded was that you're still drifting, trying to get over Winston."

"Oh. Then you've heard we're divorced."

Lindsay had the feeling he was about to say that the whole eastern seaboard had heard, but instead he replied smoothly, "I happened to run into Winston one weekend at a yachting event."

"Oh, I see." With enormous relief, Lindsay spotted Steven making his way toward them. "Well, I'm loving it here. This farm once belonged to my grandfather. It belongs now to this gentleman." She reached out and took Steven's arm, feeling as her fingers curved over his warmth that she was safe again. Though safe from what, she wasn't quite sure.

"Steven," she said, "I'd like you to meet Jonathon Page, an old friend and a successful New York lyricist. Jonathon, this is Steven Strake. He's the winemaker here." She smiled up at him. "And a Harvard lawyer."

The two men shook hands. Then Jonathon said with a sardonic twist of his lips, "That's an interesting combination of professions, Strake. Did I miss your shingle tacked up somewhere while I was touring?"

Steven's cool gaze traveled over him. "I'm not practicing at the moment." Turning back to Lindsay, he said, "What I am doing is draining vats." For her, he had the special smile that always turned her knees to water. "You're on, little one, in the morning at eight."

Lindsay could almost see Jonathon's ears perking up at Steven's husky tone of endearment. Hurriedly she said, "I have a very responsible job here, Jonathon, but I have to be coaxed into doing it."

She saw Steven frown and squeezed his arm reassuringly. But at the same time she felt as if she were juggling more balls than she could keep in the air. "I'm climbing into one of Steven's vats in the morning for the first time. To clean it. The entry hole is about as big around as a coffee canister, and he's afraid if he's not nice to me, I'll change my mind."

Steven's glance cut into her. "That's your privilege, anytime you choose." He disengaged his arm. "Excuse me," he said, and walked away.

"Touchy fellow," Jonathon remarked mildly. "How long have you worked for him?"

"Long enough to know he isn't touchy at all." But at once Lindsay regretted her sharp reply. "I'm sorry, Jonathon." She managed a smile. "I didn't mean to be snappish." Jonathon was a good friend. She had learned a lot from him at Boston U and she had heard reports of his success in Paris. It wasn't surprising that he was in New York and doing well. He deserved recognition. She thought suddenly how lucky it was that he was here. He could criticize her song.

But more important just now was seeing if she could mend her fences with Steven. She said to Jonathon, "I think I was tactless, too, with my remark about the vats. Can you stay where you are for a minute? I'll be right back." She started off and then turned around again. "You aren't with one of the bus tours, are you?"

"Oh, heavens, no," he replied. "I have my own car."

"Good." That settled it then. "I want you to stay for supper."

She went in search of Steven and found him checking the afternoon's wine sales in his office in the main room. He glanced up when she came in. "Is your friend gone?"

"No, he isn't. I've asked him to eat with us." She stopped beside the desk. "You don't mind, do you?"

"It's too bad if I do, isn't it?"

"Steven!"

He leveled his gaze at her. "I got your message back there, loud and clear. You'd rather Jonathon Page didn't know that our relationship has gone a little beyond a business association." He turned back to his books. "I think it might be better if I have supper at my own house."

"Steven—he's a friend that Winston and I knew in college. He still sees Winston, and he's something of a gossip. I certainly don't care what Winston thinks, but on general principles I'd rather Jonathon didn't give him any juicy tidbits to speculate on and spread around."

Steven's chin jutted. "Then eat with Jonathon by yourself."

Her face flooded with color. "He's not one of your moon-and-June rhymers! I want him to hear my song because he's an astute critic." She dropped her eyes. "And I want you there to hold my hand under the table if he tells me it's no good."

"It seems to me the important thing is whether *you* think it's any good." Steven's steady gaze bored into her. "Unless you're hoping he'll find a spot for you in New York."

Lindsay trembled. Why was he bringing up the subject of her returning to a full-time musical career when she had dismissed it as something too far down the road to discuss? But his insistent gaze made her reiterate her stand. "New York is something I'm looking forward to eventually, but for now, this is where I want to be."

"You may feel differently if Page likes your song."

The peace and security Lindsay had been basking in all day seemed to be eroding at a frightening rate. "I won't feel differently," she said staunchly. "Being here—with you—is too important to me."

"It's entirely your decision." But Lindsay noted with relief that the edge was gone from his voice. In a minute he closed the ledger and looked up, a faint smile beginning on his lips. "It was people like Jonathon Page who helped me make up my mind to leave Manhattan. But if it's important to you, I guess I can stand him for one evening."

"How can you possibly know what he's like?" She smiled her relief. "You didn't say three words to each other."

Steven answered dryly, "Two were enough." But he took her elbow and moved with her toward the door.

However, Lindsay observed that when they were out in the tasting room in sight of Jonathon, he was careful not to touch her again.

8

LINDSAY was thankful that the casserole she had made during one of her lonely evenings and set out to thaw before the picnic, was large enough to accommodate another appetite in addition to Steven's and her own. She stuck the dish in the oven and began tossing a salad, thinking with relief how well the two men seemed to be getting along in the parlor.

Then to her dismay she heard Jonathon call out, "What strange gnomish furniture, Lindsay. Where on earth did you get it?"

Before she could think of a tactful answer, Steven put in coldly, "An uncle of mine made it." He paused and Lindsay felt the steel in his silence. "The Peabody Museum in Salem has made a number of offers for it."

Unimpressed, Jonathon answered, "That's really where it belongs, isn't it."

Lindsay poked her head out of the kitchen and glared at Jonathon. "I'm grateful that Steven was wise enough to keep it. Otherwise I would have missed out on a great deal of pleasure. I adore it."

"Really?" Jonathon shrugged. "Well, everyone to his own tastes." He turned from Lindsay to Steven, who was eyeing him stonily from the sofa. "I only meant that it's not the sort of thing I would have expected Lindsay to have in her home. But then I'm forgetting. This is only a temporary home, isn't it?"

Steven said, "It's Lindsay's for as long as she wants it."

"I see." He raised his voice to carry out to the kitchen where Lindsay, grinding her teeth, stood by the stove. "By the way, Lindsay, how soon are you planning to come to New York?"

Lindsay replied crossly, "You sound as if I told you I meant to, Jonathon."

"I think you might have," he said pointedly, "if we'd had a few more minutes of uninterrupted talk. But surely you do have in mind a move to the city. Where else can you find a proper outlet for your talent?"

"I'm not giving much thought to music at the moment, Jonathon."

"Why ever not?"

"Steven," Lindsay called out firmly, "pour Jonathon another glass of sherry, will you? And I think he might enjoy taking a look at that book of photographs that Rachel left, the one showing the history of the vineyard."

She hurried with her dinner preparations after that, burning the casserole on the edges in her haste to get it done sooner. During the meal she kept Jonathon talking about his experiences in Paris so that Steven's brooding silence was not so noticeable.

But afterward, when they were sitting in her "gnomish" chairs with glasses of after-dinner wine and Lindsay was trying to think of how best to reintroduce the subject of her music, Steven startled her by turning to Jonathon with an invitation.

"Before you go, Page, you might like to stop off at my house. I have a piano, and Lindsay's written something I think you should hear."

"Is that so?" Jonathon was instantly attentive. "How interesting."

Watching him tense as he set aside his glass, Lindsay felt the same rush of excitement that she had experienced the first time she heard one of her pieces played before an audience.

"I knew you couldn't mean it, Lindsay, when you said you weren't thinking about music. It would have been easier to believe that you'd given up breathing."

Lindsay flushed at the accuracy of his statement. "I've written only this one song."

Jonathon got to his feet. "Well, by all means, let's go and hear it."

"Yes," Steven remarked dryly, "since that's what you were hoping for when you took Sunday off to drive to Connecticut."

"Steven," Lindsay rebuked, "Jonathon came to see the winery."

"That's true, Strake," Jonathon answered easily. "But a mutual acquaintance did happen to mention that one of your tour guides might be someone I knew." He smiled benignly at Lindsay. "Susan, I think it was."

Susan Fields, her old roommate. The only Long Island friend to whom Lindsay had given her Connecticut address. They had all been part of the same crowd at the university. Apparently Jonathon had very much wanted to get in touch or he wouldn't have gone to the trouble of polling their shared acquaintances to find out where she was. Her heartbeat accelerated. He might have a show in mind . . . was he looking for someone to write the score?

On the way up the hill to Steven's house, Lindsay's thoughts raced. What was the next step if Jonathon liked her song? Should she let him take it with him? What was Steven thinking now, trudging along beside her? How generous he'd been, she reflected, volunteering his piano even though it meant prolonging an evening he hadn't enjoyed.

She cast a grateful glance at his craggy profile. Despite the misgivings stirred up earlier by his remarks about her being a composer, Steven had shown this evening that he respected her talent, that he cared about her career. He would never be guilty of imposing the kind of selfish restrictions that had made life with Winston unendurable. Steven and Winston were nothing alike. Why had she ever worried?

IN THE PARLOR of the farmhouse, Steven settled himself in his favorite chair by the fire. Jonathon took the Queen Anne rocker opposite him and faced the piano. And Lindsay put her fingers to the keyboard.

In a moment the sweet lilting music poured out and swept through the rooms of the old house. The only other sound while she played was the sigh of a spent log shattering into a million sparks on the hearth.

Then the music stopped, and there was no sound at all for so long that Lindsay clenched her hands in her lap and felt ill, waiting for Jonathon to say something ... anything at all that would put an end to the unbearable suspense that gripped her.

Finally it was Steven who spoke. "Well?" he demanded harshly. "What do you think?"

Jonathon reacted to his menacing tone with a bemused glance. "What could I think, except that it's wonderful. Lindsay's music is always wonderful. I don't know of anyone who can touch her when it comes to balance and poignancy. This piece has everything. Spirit, passion." He got up. "The only fault I can hear is a slight limpness at the midpoint."

At Lindsay's crestfallen look following such praise, he strode briskly to the piano. "It's nothing we can't fix, though. Here, move over, I'll show you."

She slid along the bench, and he put his

fingers on the keys. "Let's try the refrain in a minor key and see what happens."

For a few minutes there was nothing but a grating jumble of sounds that made Steven tighten his jaw and glare at the two figures on the piano bench, but in another minute a wistful new variation began to flow.

Lindsay turned to Jonathon with sparkling eyes. "Yes, yes! The contrast is marvelous! You're a genius, Jonathon!"

"No, you're the genius," he answered bluntly. "I'm only a salt and pepper man who has a sixth sense for adding the spice. I can't write music." He eyed her sternly. "But you can. And every minute that you're not doing it is wasted."

Lindsay was conscious of Steven's silence in the background. "I'll get back to it one of these days. I'm just not ready yet."

"Not ready," Jonathon snorted. "You can say that after you've written this piece of music? Look here—" He reached for his jacket lying nearby on the sofa. From one of its pockets he pulled a sheaf of typewritten pages. "I've been studying a marvelous script by a fellow from the Northwest. These are several sets of lyrics I've derived from it. Try out this one on your tune."

Lindsay took the page he handed her. Bright spots of color stood high on her cheeks and her breath came unevenly as she pored over the words Jonathon had written. "They're lovely, Jonathon," she said at last. "Certainly we share the same feeling for tempo. Maybe if we interchanged these first two lines and then brought this one up from the bottom—"

An hour ticked by on the mantel clock. All at once Lindsay remembered Steven. She spun around on the bench, dreading the sight of his empty chair.

But he was still there, his fingers steepled beneath his chin, his blue-eyed gaze telling her nothing.

"Oh, Steven! We're boring you senseless, aren't we?"

He answered dryly, "I still have a few wits about me. Enough at least to know that I've had a front row seat at the conception of a Broadway show."

Jonathon's eyes lighted up with the first show of respect for Steven. "You're damned right you have. Unless I badly miss my guess, we have a super hit on our hands."

Lindsay stared. "We've got one song!"

"And the lyrics for six others," Jonathon replied, unperturbed. "All we're lacking is the music. And that's your department. How about it?" The directness of his gaze made her quiver. "Will you stop playing hard to get and come to New York so we can get started?"

Panic gripped her. "When?"

"Now." He threw up his hands. "Next

week." Sardonically he added, "Or as soon as you can resign your position here."

Lindsay was aware of Steven's gaze boring into her and of her own pounding heart. "Jonathon, I'm not ready for what you're proposing."

"Good grief, Lindsay! What do I have to do, set off a case of dynamite under you? I tell you, we've got something special here. Steven can see it, why can't you? We can seize this moment and fly. Or we can wait another five years for a chance half as promising—if we're lucky."

"You're dramatizing the situation."

"That's what show business is all about—drama! Well?" Eagerness made the word rasp in his throat. "What do you say?"

Lindsay glanced once, quickly, at Steven. The expressionless mask he wore revealed nothing of what he was thinking, but she knew she had never loved him more, or wanted him more. Or been more icily afraid that she was about to lose him.

She pulled in her breath and turned back to Jonathon. "No."

"*No!*" Jonathon stared at her in disbelief. "Give me one plausible reason why not?"

"I don't want to, that's all. Not now." She clenched her hands together in her lap. "When I do—if I do—I'll get in touch with you."

Jonathon got up off the bench and pulled on

his jacket. "By that time, I'll have signed with somebody else."

Lindsay tossed her hair over her shoulder. "Then I guess that's a chance I'll just have to take."

"THAT WAS some performance," Steven said mildly as they watched from the gate as the taillights of Jonathon's silver Mercedes bounced along the gravel road toward the highway.

"Whose?" Lindsay said absently. "His or mine?"

"Both of you seemed like award winners to me."

Lindsay sighed, still numb from turning down what might have been the chance of a lifetime. "Jonathon has been in New York too long."

"My sentiments exactly. But I'm surprised that you're sharing them."

Lindsay brought her head around. "Actually, I'm not. I don't think that even you can deny that New York has its place on a larger scale than we're used to. Things happen there that can't happen anywhere else in the world."

Steven put his arm around her waist and walked her back toward the house. "Like hit musicals that are born in Connecticut farmhouses?"

"Jonathon was dreaming in that regard. Even if I'd agreed to collaborate with him, we're light-years away from a hit."

Steven shook his head. "As annoying as I find your friend, I think he knows what he's talking about. But he needs your music to make it happen. And he's not going to give up until he has it."

"You're wrong. He wouldn't have allowed himself to get angry if that were the case. He would have stayed and pressured me more."

"He threatened you instead. He's a smart man. He'll give you time now to make up your own mind, to decide you want to join him."

They climbed the steps, and Steven opened the door for them to pass through the hall and into the cozy parlor again. Jonathon's sheaf of lyrics lay on the coffee table, and Steven pointed them out. "You see? He left his calling card."

He turned the pages over and took them from the table. "Every sheet has his telephone number and address stamped on it to make it easy for you when you're ready to contact him." Steven turned around suddenly. "You wanted to say yes tonight, Lindsay. Why didn't you?"

Startled, she stared back at him. "I'm not ready to go to New York."

"So I heard you tell Page."

"I told you the same thing this afternoon."

"The situation has changed since then." Then in a gesture that seemed overly casual, he dropped the lyrics back down on the table. "Never mind. It's entirely your business."

She moved quickly to his side. "The same way that your sitting up half the night studying Supreme Court cases is your business? Is that what you're saying?"

"Something like that."

"Steven—" A few minutes ago her musical future had hung in the balance. For the time being, she had decided in favor of Steven, but now it seemed to her that it might be possible to speed up her hopes for the two of them going to New York. She hesitated a moment longer, and then decided to take the plunge. "Steven, have you ever thought how much fun it might be if one of these days you decided to go back to Dexter, Brink and Dexter, and at the same time I—"

She got no further. Steven reached out and crooked a finger under her chin. "Lindsay—" his blue eyes darkened "—I am never going to do that."

Her heart pounded. "But you can't deny that you're still crazy about the law."

"I'm crazy about watching grapes ripen on the vine and the way the sun comes up over Havelock Hill." He gazed down at her with unwavering firmness. "I'm crazy about watching the leaves turn in the fall, and I like to wake up on a moonlit night and see the skeletons of trees silhouetted against sky instead of buildings."

She choked out, frightfully close to tears, "And your precious stars. Don't forget them."

"Lindsay, if you want to go to New York, nobody's stopping you."

You're stopping me! she wanted to shout. A month ago, standing with him in front of her cottage, if she had known she was going to fall in love with him, she would have left. She would have run down the road with her coat-tails flying. But now it was too late. Tonight had made her realize how important it was to be where there were people like Jonathon Page, where there were producers to turn her dreams into realities, and limitless possibilities to fulfill her potential. It was true she was still limping, not quite recuperated, not quite cured of her sense of homelessness and the damage Winston had done. But she could make it now, she could grow stronger with every success . . . if only she didn't have to leave Steven.

As if he read her mind, he pulled her into his arms and said gently, "But if you decide to stay on here, the piano is yours whenever you want it. If I'm not here, it doesn't matter. You know where the key is."

Listening to his tender murmur, Lindsay saw herself poised on the edge of a precipice. Then Steven brought his mouth down on hers. The powerful pull of his sexuality invaded her lips and spread out to her limbs and down through her body. His hands encircling her waist, fitting her snugly to his body, roused the desire that with catlike patience had toler-ated the proceedings of the evening, knowing with a primitive instinct that when all was said and done, it was Steven's embrace that would count above everything else.

He whispered against her cheek, "Tomorrow is your big day. Do you want me to walk you home?"

"No...." She clung to him, intoxicating herself with the scent of his skin and its salty taste on her tongue. "What I want is for you to make love to me."

"Ah, well...." His thickened voice smoldered huskily in her ear. "Why didn't you say so, lady?" Lifting her in his arms, he turned toward the stairs.

9

THE ROOM Steven chose for their lovemaking was a small dormer room that had once served Lindsay's grandfather as an office and now was Steven's study. Before, when she had come upstairs with Steven, the door was always closed. It was closed when they reached it this time, but Steven opened it, and in the darkness as his hand went out for the light switch, the smell of leather and old bookbindings and fine, mellowing paper reached her nostrils.

When the light came on, a disorderly desk, two chairs piled with law books, and a long, low couch like a wide window seat sprang out of the shadows.

"This is your hideaway," Lindsay said in an awed whisper against his neck, and a thrill ran through her. For the first time Steven was admitting her into the most private area of his life, the area that meant to him what music meant to her.

He laid her gently on the couch. Through the dormer window, she saw the stars he loved so, twinkling like bits of white ice in the velvet sky.

"How special," she murmured. She was tingling all over in anticipation of his touch, yearning for him, as he moved back toward the door.

"I'll get the light," he said, and once more the room was dark. She heard him coming toward her again. "Sometimes I leave books all over the floor," he explained. "I'd have hated ramming into six volumes of jurisprudence and breaking your beautiful neck."

And then he was reaching for her, nimbly opening her shirt, sliding it off her shoulders. His warm hands cupped her breasts, his mouth kissed them. Then breathlessly, hurriedly they undressed each other. The friction of bare flesh made Steven mutter, "Was it only this afternoon I held you?"

"It was more like a hundred years ago." She recalled the yellow daisies in the cream pitcher that morning, and Eleanor and Dr. White. How could she ever leave this place? Leave Steven? She pressed against him, needing his touch. The clean, sharp scent of his shaving lotion mingled with the masculine smell of the leather beneath them. She felt him hardening against her, the taut muscles of his thighs binding her to him. Was there ever an ecstasy to compare with this?

She gave a little cry and opened to him, and then there was the furious unleashing of all they had held back through the long evening. In Steven's arms she found a rapture that

made everything else pale to insignificance.
She heard his moans and clasped him tighter,
soaring in the joy his pleasure brought her.

"Steven, Steven—"

Their ecstasy peaked, ripped through them
and then ebbed, slowly, gloriously. Lindsay
imagined there were gold coins dancing in her
bloodstream, flashing their golden sides as
they bobbed along through all the intricate
passages of her body, gilding her...making
her shimmer inside and out....

She let out a long sigh and stretched lux-
uriously against Steven's damp heated form.
"You're a magician," she said with a pixie
smile. "You make me over every time into the
national treasury." She drew a finger down
the glistening path of hair that grew to his
navel. "After you've loved me, I have gold in
my veins and diamonds on the tip of my
tongue."

He hugged her and said in a low voice,
"Show me."

Her laughter held the sound of gold, too, a
merry, tinkling sound that was muffled in the
hollow of his shoulder. "You're greedy, Steven
Strake."

"Greedy for you, always." He smoothed the
tapering lines of her backside with sensitive
fingers. She shivered from the sensations he
produced and coiled against him again.

He nibbled at her lips. "Winston West was a
damned fool, but I'm grateful to him."

Lying secure in Steven's arms, rich with the moments they had just shared, she thought sadly of her former husband. "I'm afraid I haven't always been fair when I've talked about Winston."

Steven groaned. "You've convinced me that he's a monster. You aren't going to disillusion me, are you?"

But he saw at once how serious Lindsay was. He let her go and she turned over on her side to rest her temple on the heel of one hand. The starlight coming through the dormer showed Steven's expectant, craggy face, poised for whatever she was going to say.

"Ever since we broke up I've laid all the blame on him for our problems." She paused. "I thought for a long time that's where it belonged, but recently, *since you taught me how to love, Steven,* I've realized that I was at fault, too. It's true that he had an affair that crushed and humiliated me, that damaged my confidence in myself as a desirable woman—"

Steven leaned closer and kissed away a strand of hair that lay along her cheekbone. "So far, so good," he murmured. "He's exactly the idiot I thought he was."

But Lindsay persisted. "It's true he did all those things. But they were secondary to the real reason I left him. Eventually, if I'd tried, perhaps I could have adjusted even to infidelity." She paused, wanting to be sure she told the truth this time, to herself as well as to

Steven. "It was the way he felt about my music that I couldn't forgive, that was unendurable."

Steven inquired quietly, "How did he feel about your music?"

"He came to consider it an enemy. He felt that it intruded on our marriage in a way he couldn't tolerate. For Winston, a day without parties and yachting was wasted. He believed that the hours I spent at the piano were an excuse to avoid going with him to the places that bored me."

"Was he right?"

"He was right that I was bored with a lot of the things that amused him. But I never used music for an excuse. I was seriously—desperately—trying to work."

"Then you mustn't blame yourself."

"I was at fault in another way." She hesitated, aware that this was untried ground she'd never felt brave enough to test. "I knew Winston felt in competition with my music. I could have made it easier for him if I had wanted badly enough to save our marriage. If I had cared enough to want to stay with him, I needn't have been so rigidly dedicated. But I kept on insisting that he view my ability to compose as an extension of myself. It angered me that he thought he could have me in his life and not have my music, too. It angered *him* that anything of so little importance could matter to me more than he did. The scores I was writing, he told me, weren't worth the paper they were written on."

Steven was firmly reassuring. "You knew he was wrong."

But Lindsay shook her head again. "I knew he was right. And that was the basic fault of our marriage. The life we were trying to share stifled me. It blocked my creativity. The more he goaded me, the more stilted and cold my compositions became. The more stilted and cold *I* became." A shiver ran through her. "Winston retaliated with an affair. And I divorced him."

It was the first time she had ever shouldered this much blame. Talking about it was more traumatic than she had imagined. She sought shelter in Steven's arms and against his wide chest.

He gathered her to him and held her until the tension that had made her tremble drained away.

Finally she summed it all up in a small sad voice. "I married Winston for all the wrong reasons. If he turned into a monster, I helped to make him one."

Steven soothed, "You're too hard on yourself. From what you've told me, the two of you must have been incompatible from the start. Your priorities could never have meshed." He smoothed back her hair. "Winston needed a playmate. And you needed a career in music."

They were silent for a while after that, lying

quietly, at home in each other's arms. Then Lindsay, feeling washed clean clear through, commented thoughtfully, "Our needs—what amazing lengths we go to to gratify them."

"Umm," Steven agreed, tracing the outline of her mouth with the back of his thumb. "It's painfully hard work sometimes, getting what we want out of life." His hand slid down along the curve of her body to her naked hip. "But there are other moments, like this one—" he kissed her lips with lingering tenderness "—when gratifying a need is as simple as discovering that the sweetest fruit is growing on the nearest limb."

10

THE WORK at the winery grew more frenzied as the middle of November approached. There were dozens of tasks that kept the whole team busy: filtering the wine; clarifying it to bring out its finest flavors and fragrances; checking its acidity; maintaining a steady fifty-five degrees Fahrenheit in the tanks for proper fermentation. The list was endless, Lindsay soon discovered.

But her greatest challenge was mastering the art of breathing within the confines of the steel vats. At first, fits of claustrophobia sent her gasping to the small side openings. Then gradually, her distress moderated and finally faded away altogether as she learned to concentrate on Katie's lovely soprano echoing inside a nearby tank. If Katie grew lightheaded, her voice conversely soared in a manner that amazed Lindsay and delighted her trained ear.

Afterward when Lindsay marveled, Katie would laughingly tell her, "In those close quarters I sound to myself like the whole cast of a grand opera. I can't resist belting it out, even if I might faint. Steven will have to fight me if he ever wants to bar me from the tanks."

"If you love it so much," Lindsay replied dryly, "you may take my turn any day you want."

But whenever the tanks were emptied, both of them, as the two smallest members of the team, were needed for the tedious scraping of the inner surfaces before the tanks could be flushed and readied for new wine. After Katie and Lindsay had endured all they could for one session, Steven usually rewarded them with a few hours off. On those days they fell into the habit of fixing a quick lunch at Lindsay's cottage and then going up afterward to Steven's house to play the piano and sing.

No further word had come from Jonathon Page. Steven had not mentioned again Jonathon's proposal that he and Lindsay collaborate, and Lindsay was so busy and so immersed in the routine she and Steven had established that she pushed to the back of her mind all thoughts of going to New York.

Most evenings she had dinner with Steven. If she played the piano, she stuck to the classics that were his favorites, saving her own compositions for the times she was alone in the house. When their weekends were free, they took long walks or drove around the countryside in the Old Gray Mare, poking into antique barns and attending auctions. Other times they spent precious hours snuggled together in Steven's four-poster, making endless discoveries that took precedence over everything else in the world.

But Jonathon's lyrics had embedded themselves in Lindsay's subconscious. Some part of every day she found herself fitting notes to phrases she recollected while she worked. When a whole tune developed in her head she scratched it down on whatever was handy and later recopied the score in a folder she kept in her clothes closet. If Steven had heard her playing fragments from them, he never commented. The knowledge that she had a secret treasure eased her whenever nagging thoughts of passing time reminded her of the career she was neglecting.

One afternoon shortly after Thanksgiving, Steven was away on a sales promotion in Hartford, and she and Katie had the house to themselves. On an impulse Lindsay got out her folder and carried it up from the cottage.

In Steven's parlor she set it up on the piano. "Have a look at this," she said to Katie. "Some of these might be just right for your range."

Katie examined the folder curiously. "Where did you get all these songs?"

"A friend in New York wrote the lyrics. I wrote the music."

Katie was suitably awed, but when she got over her initial nervousness, she hummed through one piece several times and then, with Lindsay accompanying, sang it in the clear, lilting way that had so impressed Lindsay in the past. When they were finished, tears stood in the eyes of both of them.

"Oh, *Lindsay!*" Katie leaned against the piano. "That's so beautiful it gives me the shivers. Let's try another one!"

For an hour they were mesmerized—Katie by the bonanza of beautiful music that had suddenly dropped into her lap, and Lindsay by the stunning realization of just how good her work was, teamed up with Jonathon's.

After they had gone through the folder twice and Katie was parading around the parlor, waving the sheets of music like flags in front of her, she said to Lindsay, "Tell me what you plan to do with these."

"I don't know—nothing, maybe." A chill swept over Lindsay. "Probably the friend who wrote the lyrics has another collaborator by now." She thought dizzily of the treasure she had hoarded too long, and it made her sick to realize that there was a strong possibility no one would ever hear these songs as they were now except herself and Katie.

The same thought occurred simultaneously to Katie. "Do you mean that maybe some other songwriter has put different music to these words? Oh, Lindsay!" She gave her friend an incredulous look. "How could you let that happen?"

Lindsay wondered herself. What kind of spell had Steven cast that had made her careless enough to cheat these pieces of music out of lives of their own? She had cheated Jonathon, too, to say nothing of herself.

Breathlessly she answered Katie, "Maybe it's not too late. I have the lyricist's number. I could call him, I suppose."

"Call him now!" Katie's face glowed with excitement. "Somebody ought to be recording these gorgeous songs. Or maybe they could be a part of a show! Have you ever thought of aiming at Broadway, Lindsay?"

"Have you?" Lindsay countered.

"Only night and day for eighteen years," the girl replied. "But I've never told anyone that except you." Katie threw herself down on the sofa and held the sheets of music like lilies pressed to her breast. "I might as well dream of going to the moon, hadn't I?"

"I don't see why," said Lindsay, though her thoughts were galloping off in a different direction. "Every star on Broadway came from somewhere else. Why shouldn't one of them come from Terrapin Falls?"

Katie sat up. "Yes, why not? Except that to get a start, you need to know someone. Lucky you, you have your lyricist. Maybe you and he—" She halted suddenly. "But what about Steven?"

Lindsay's mouth went dry. "What about him?"

"You two are in love, aren't you?"

Lindsay glanced away from Katie's bright

questioning eyes. The girl's directness had ripped the covers off the two dilemmas she tried not to think about: her career and the part Steven might play in her future.

Since the night of Jonathon's visit her relationship with Steven had deepened on every plane. She felt perfectly at home now curled up in a chair in his study with a book of her own while he pored over his law books. She ran in and out of his house, using the piano whenever she wanted to. He cooked cozy dinners for her, they finished each other's sentences. But there was never any talk of love ... never any talk of what might happen to their lives beyond tomorrow.

Her heart bumped and she sat down shakily on the piano bench. "Steven and I have fun together. But we're just good friends."

Katie hooted. "Tell that to the gang at the winery. You guys are made for each other. It sticks out all over both of you."

Lindsay said stiffly, "I didn't realize we were such a topic of conversation."

Katie's face fell. "Oh, gee, have I poked my nose in where it doesn't belong? We weren't gossiping about you. Honestly, we weren't. It's just that it makes us happy to look at the two of you together." She finished in a warm burst of affection, "We've decided you ought to get married."

Lindsay forced a smile though inside she ached. "Pass the word along not to count on it," she instructed firmly. "Now come on." She got up from the bench. "I've got an hour's labeling to do before the winery closes."

Katie sighed and pulled herself off the sofa. Casting a sorrowful look at the sheets of music in her hand, she slipped them back into Lindsay's folder. "It's too bad about these songs. I hope you'll call that guy in New York, just to see what he says." She paused. "But if it comes to a toss, Lindsay—Broadway or Steven—I hope you vote for Steven."

LINDSAY HAD STEAKS coming off the grill and was mixing a cheese sauce for broccoli when Steven arrived back from Hartford. A strong north wind had blown up, and when he came into her kitchen, his nose was as red as a strawberry and the cheek he laid against hers was icy.

She clung to him, reveling in the crisp coldness his clothes gave off and the warmth that underlay them. Each time she saw him, all her senses reached out to him. Each time he touched her, she wanted to stay in his arms forever.

He kissed her forehead and smoothed back her hair. "Hello, little one, how was your day?"

Suddenly she wanted to weep. How did he always know when to deal with her gently? Jonathon was just the opposite sort of man, cutting when he thought he had the advantage. On the telephone, he had gloated. He had two other composers interested in his lyrics, he informed her. One was ready to sign with him in the morning. But he supposed he might hold off, maybe for a day, if Lindsay was sure she had something worthwhile to show him.

"Did you miss me?" Steven nuzzled her neck.

"Terribly." She closed her eyes and held him tight. "It was a long day."

"What did you do?"

She hedged. "Just routine things. And Katie and I fooled around at the piano. She has a wonderful voice, Steven."

"Wonderful," he agreed and teased her with his lips. "Do you have a kiss for me?"

"I have dozens and dozens."

His mouth turning on hers was warm... soft and firm, velvet and steel... a paradox of wonders that made her forget the broccoli until it was boiling over and smelling up the kitchen.

While she tended to the cleaning up, Steven dipped a finger into the cheese sauce. "What have we here, something new?"

"I cut the recipe out of Sunday's paper. How did your trip go? Did you make any sales?"

"My dear," he answered loftily, "do birds have wings?"

She heard the excitement beneath his banter, and guessing the source of it, whirled around. "Don't tell me—Annabelle bought all the Seyval Blanc!"

She was rewarded by a wide grin. "Right you are. All two hundred and thirty-eight cases." He caught her by the waist and lifted her high. "What's more, she's coming to the winery in a few days to taste the Marechal Foch I'm bringing out of oak. If she likes it, we're going to make a special label and she'll buy the whole yield. We'll be grossing thirty percent over last year, even before Christmas."

"Oh, Steven! All your news is wonderful!"

At once he was alert to the tremor that ran beneath her jubilance. "Isn't yours?" he asked casually as he set her down.

"What makes you think I have any?" She busied herself sliding the steaks onto a platter.

"Because you're tossing your hair around, Your Highness." He pulled out her chair at the table. "You haven't done that since Jonathon Page was here badgering you."

She raised her smoky eyes to his. "Funny you should mention Jonathon."

A watchful look cloaked his eyes. "Was he here again today?"

"No." She moistened her lips. "But I talked to him on the telephone—at length." She made her tone very light, very airy. "The toll will show up on your bill, sir."

"Fine." He matched her airiness. "I'll take it out of your next check, madam."

But after that, he ate in silence, asking none of the questions she expected and had braced herself to answer. She pushed her food around on her plate and listened to the wind. She was reminded of the silent dinners she had sat through with Winston, and her stomach knotted.

But finally they began to talk of other things. The BMW needed a new set of tires. Snow was predicted for Vermont.

Then on the sofa in the parlor, sitting close together with a relaxed mood reestablished between them, Steven said out of the blue, "When are you going to New York?"

At once she was defensive. "I haven't said I was."

"But it's obvious that you are."

She bristled. "And it's obvious that if I do, you won't like it."

"New York," he said with a casual air of dismissal. "It's too far away." He put his arm around her and pulled her against his chest. "This is where I like for you to be." He brought his mouth down. "As close as breath, as near as a kiss." As soon as his lips touched hers, Lindsay felt the jittery uncertainty of the afternoon draining away.

"But if you have to go," he sighed, "you have to go."

She nestled against him. "Maybe I'll mail what I have to Jonathon."

"And maybe you won't. You might as well admit that you've been dying to strike out for the big city for weeks."

It irked her that now he seemed too willing

to let her go. But he was again the Steven she adored, gently mocking and terribly sexual in his quiet gaiety. She knew that beneath his lightheartedness, strong virile currents were churning, and when he unleashed them, nothing could compare with the ecstasy they could arouse. "I don't *have* to go, Steven."

"You have to if you want to." Prickles of desire ran up her spine in response to his hand stroking her nape. "It amounts to the same thing."

She leaned into his chest and traced the outline of his mouth with her fingertips. "I also want to be with you."

"Ah," he intoned solemnly. "Behold the maiden pinned on the horns of the dilemma. Will she stay? Will she go?"

"If I do go," she whispered, "I'll be gone for only a few days."

He kissed her lips and let his mouth linger. "One day is too long."

She teased, "You'll have Annabelle while I'm away as a nice diversion."

"Oh, yes, I forgot about Annabelle." He grew playfully ferocious, growling against her throat. "I'll ravish her in the corking room, and she'll be so grateful, she'll buy the whole winery, and I shall retire to live happily ever after on truffle foie gras in her elegant Hartford salon."

Lindsay laughed and said, only half teasing now, "Tell me not to go, Steven, and I'll stay."

A sober tone came into his voice. "I'd never tell you that, Lindsay. You have to do whatever you think is best."

For a moment she wished he were as demanding and unreasonable as Winston had been. She wished he would lay down a flat ultimatum: *Don't go or else.* As soon as he did, she would hate it, of course, but at least she would know he shared her fear that this first step away from him might be the beginning of the end. As it was, all he had given her was his blessing. "Sometimes you're too agreeable," she told him curtly.

"Am I?" He reached down and brought her chin up. "Why?" His eyes searched hers for a clue to her mood change. "Would you rather I kept you in chains?"

Half a dozen answers trembled on her lips, but she held them back. The freedom she enjoyed in their relationship was what she preferred, of course. Her marriage to Winston had been positive proof that one person's effort to control another was no indication of love. That she had wished it were just now, even for an instant, showed how desperate she was for Steven to declare himself. Irked again, she tossed her head defensively.

"Even if you tried, I would never allow you to keep me in chains." But she couldn't help adding, "However, it's not very flattering that you're so eager for me to go."

"The sooner you go," he murmured sooth

ingly, "the sooner you'll be back. Besides, it's not as if you were going away forever. You'll be in New York two or three days, and then you'll be home."

Home. Lindsay glanced at him quickly, wondering if he realized how his use of that word committed him. But nothing in his blandly confident expression indicated that he did.

She moved out of his embrace. "It may take as long as a week," she said with studied carelessness. "Jonathon thinks we should see several producers."

He watched her walk across the room to pull down the shades on the small windows that fronted the cottage. "You've written some new songs, haven't you?"

She swung around. "If you knew, why didn't you say something?"

He met her gaze evenly. "Why didn't you play them for me?"

"I wanted to, Steven." She realized suddenly that this was true, but she hadn't trusted him enough. A pang of regret stabbed her at this lost opportunity to have shared something precious. "We've been so happy. I was afraid I might spoil things."

He got up from the sofa and came toward her. "How could beautiful music spoil anything for us?" He took her in his arms. "I'm Steven," he murmured against her hair. "Winston is out of the picture, remember?"

Gratefully she nestled against the solid wall of his chest. "Keep reminding me, will you?"

He kissed the top of her head and then led her toward the door. "Come on. Let's go up to the house. You have a piano recital long overdue."

LINDSAY PLAYED for three quarters of an hour in the cozy ambience of Steven's parlor. She missed the exuberance of Katie's lilting voice, but without the vocal accompaniment, she could hear more clearly the subtleties of the compositions. By the time she was finished playing, Lindsay was instinctively certain of success in New York. There was a polished professional quality in everything she had written. When she turned away from the keyboard at last, Steven's smile told her that he agreed.

"To quote your friend Jonathon," he said, "I think you have six hits on your hands."

She came to his chair and perched on the arm. "Katie tried them out with the lyrics this afternoon." She spoke shyly, but her eyes were sparkling. "They did sound wonderful, Steven."

"Of course they're wonderful. You're a wonderful composer." He gazed up at her and his blue eyes seemed bottomless. "Someday I'll be able to say, 'I knew her when.'"

Lindsay's throat constricted. Where would

the two of them be then? Together? Or would she be a world apart from Steven ... and miles from this comfortable old house that held so many memories, old and new?

Musing, she felt his hand on her spine. Its circular sensuous strokings awoke an irresistible desire. Sliding down into his lap, she forgot the songs she had written. She forgot everything except Steven's lips closing over hers, and the quivering, eager response of her body to his kiss.

In the closeness of the chair, the flow of power along Steven's muscular hardness was more intense, more urgent than ever before. A raging excitement seized Lindsay. With a hasty fumbling awkwardness they came out of their clothes, permitting the fullness and depth of caresses that were bound by no restraints, permitting the hot union for which their flesh clamored.

Within moments their passion peaked. A muffled cry broke from Steven's throat. "Lindsay—" He kneaded the silky skin of her back with feverish intensity, his voice thickening on her name. And then in a spiraling upward surge of release they reached the pinnacle of fulfillment.

"Oh, Steven—" Lindsay lay back in his arms, glorying in the shimmering ecstasy that spread through her body, the shower of gold that danced through her bloodstream. Raining damp kisses on his naked shoulder, Lindsay thought of a cocoon. Their own safe steamy cocoon where nothing mattered except that they were together.

For a time they drifted in a hazy daze, mumbling the sweetnesses that their haste to be in each other's arms had precluded.

Then too soon, Steven stirred. He caressed the inviting swell of her breasts, first with knowing, skillful hands, then with his lips. Then he sighed and said, "Back to my original question ... when are you leaving for New York?"

Reluctantly, Lindsay let the real world in. She threaded her fingers through the gleaming mat of hair that covered his chest. As long as she lived, she thought, she would never get enough of touching him. "Tomorrow, I guess."

"Shall I take you to Hartford to catch the train?"

"If you like. If you're sure that you don't mind my going."

"I do mind." He held her close again and buried his face in the flowery freshness of her hair. "Tomorrow night I'll be in this chair by myself."

Her heart thudded painfully. "Is that your only reason for wanting me to stay?"

"Do you know a better one?"

She did, one that would last them for the rest of their lives. She held tightly to his shoulders, hoping he would think of it, too. But when he said nothing more, she climbed out of his arms and let him dress her by the firelight, indulging him in the languorous sensual ceremony that had always thrilled her until tonight.

Later, between the chill sheets in her cottage, she ached with thoughts of their parting. When would it occur to Steven that, like sand filtering through an hourglass, their time was running out? Or had it already occurred to him, and he was willing to let it happen?

She fell into a troubled sleep with no way to find the answers to her questions.

LINDSAY spent four days in New York. When she stepped off the train in Hartford the next Wednesday night and saw Steven climbing out of the Old Gray Mare, she was struck by the way everything seemed to be happening in slow motion, compared to the hustle and bustle of New York. Watching Steven stroll leisurely toward her, she was reminded sharply that the exhilarating pace and the excitement of the past few days were behind her.

But then he was enfolding her in his arms, and the deeply satisfying kiss he gave her told her at once that this was where she belonged.

"How did you know which train to meet?" she inquired breathlessly when he let her go at last.

"Mental telepathy," he joked. But as he was tossing her bag in the back seat of the car, he added casually, "I had to drive into Hartford this evening to deliver some wine to Annabelle. I thought I might as well drop by here, just on the chance that you could have taken this train."

His response was far from the romantic

answer Lindsay longed to hear, but settling herself on the front seat, she reflected a little smugly that there was nothing casual in the way he was dressed, or in the way he had kissed her either. She wouldn't be too surprised if he had met several trains in her absence.

Reassured, she smiled and touched his cheek when he slid under the wheel. "Annabelle took the Marechal Foch, then?"

He nodded. "The whole yield."

"That's marvelous, Steven!"

But his mind was more on her than on his booming wine business. "I missed you," he murmured, and dropped another kiss on her lips before he headed the BMW out into the early-evening traffic.

Lindsay watched the lights of Hartford go by the window. She had missed him, too, with a keenness that didn't bear thinking about too much, especially in her hotel room at the end of each day. Silence had closed around her then, and she had ached for his solid strength, his voice in her ear, his hand stroking her nape. Behind her eyelids, she had conjured up his roughly hewed face. She had hugged her pillow until she fell asleep.

But during the day there had hardly been time to think of anything except the hours at the piano with Jonathon and the whirlwind of appointments and mad dashings around town.

In the elegant restaurant where Steven took her for a drink after they left the train station, she told him exuberantly, "I'd forgotten how stimulating New York can be!"

Steven made a wry face. "Yes—wondering how many times you might be mugged before sundown."

"Oh, Steven, you're impossibly biased!" She sipped from the champagne he had ordered to celebrate her return. "There's so much to do in New York. We went twice to the theater and saw two wonderful shows. And the museums— oh, I've missed the museums! At the Guggenheim they're showing Matisse." She sighed. "All those lovely landscapes. I'm still seeing the colors."

Steven said dryly, "I thought the purpose of your trip was to see about your songs."

"Well, of course it was." She steepled her fingers beneath sparkling eyes. "That's the best news of all."

Steven showed the first real interest in what she was saying. "You sold your songs?"

She shook her head regretfully. "Not yet. Not quite. But we have a promising nibble. When the details are worked out, Jonathon will call me. The script he's working from is marvelous, Steven. And the author is a fantastic person, even more creative than Jonathon, if you can imagine. But a steadier sort. One who'll be able to work well with a producer." She laid fingers icy with excitement on

Steven's wrist. "And I think we do have a producer! I took along two letters of introduction that I brought from California. Jonathon was impressed by that, I can tell you! My stock went up ten points at least." She went on, sparing none of the details. "The producer who is the most interested is young, but he has an impressive list of backers and two hit shows to his credit." She took another sip of champagne. "Let me see if I can name them." Then suddenly she became aware that Steven had stopped listening.

"Am I boring you, Steven?"

He brought his gaze up guiltily from the menu. "Oh, sorry. I thought we might have dinner here."

"I *am* boring you." She wilted visibly. "I thought you'd be interested in what's been happening to me."

He laid the menu aside and took her hand. "So far I haven't heard much about you."

A rueful little smile turned up her lips. "I *have* been running on rather thoughtlessly, haven't I?" She sat back in her chair and gazed at him apologetically. "Lindsay Hancock is a babbling brook rushing pell-mell to the Atlantic Ocean."

A twinkle came into his eyes. "And gathering no moss on the way." He reached across the table and took her hands in his again. "But I'm glad you had a good time."

"You just don't want to hear about it."

"I do—in small, infrequent doses at well-spaced intervals. Especially the parts about Jonathon." He studied her shapely fingertips. "Anyway, I want to talk about myself."

Lindsay blinked, a little miffed. She took her hands away. "Go ahead. The floor is yours."

He brought his gaze up. "I can't eat," he said. "I can't sleep."

"What's happened?" She leaned forward, her annoyance forgotten. "Are you ill?"

"Worse than that. I'm a basket case."

"Steven! What's wrong?"

"Four days of knocking around by myself in a haunted house," he said solemnly. "I have piles of soggy dish towels all over the kitchen counters. Your chair at the table is always empty, to say nothing of the one in the parlor. I can't read my law books in all that silence. Even Eleanor and Dr. White have been moping in the sink since Sunday, waiting for your friendly hands to give them a soaping." He stared at her accusingly. "You ran my life aground and then you took a train and left me foundering with the wreckage."

Lindsay sucked in her breath. "You charlatan! You scared me half to death!"

"Good. You deserve to suffer."

She focused on his woebegone look of self-righteousness, and felt a joyous hope begin to pump through her veins. A wicked smile played on her lips. "You forgot to mention the state of the four-poster."

"It's disgustingly pristine," he answered dolefully. "Not a wrinkle on the counterpane. I sleep on the floor. It's less lonely down there."

"Steven—" Her smoky eyes began to glow. "Would it be terribly gauche to walk out of this elegant place without ordering dinner?"

His gaze leaped from her eyes to her parted lips. "Do you want to?" he asked thickly.

"Yes, please." She took his outstretched hand. "Let's go home as fast as Stepping Sam can take us."

THERE WERE hothouse flowers in all the main rooms of the clapboard farmhouse when Steven unlocked the door. A heavenly pink cyclamen greeted them from the piano top. A huge pot of varicolored primroses bloomed on the kitchen table, and up in Steven's bedroom the scent of a dozen red roses permeated their lovemaking.

Finally hunger drove them down to the kitchen where Lindsay noticed for the first time how orderly everything was. No cups in the sink. No soggy dish towels on the cabinet tops as previously proclaimed.

She stood in the middle of the room. "What's happened to this place?"

Steven took eggs and butter out of the refrigerator, which was admirably tidy, too. "First a four-day tornado hit it." He shoved back his tousled hair. "And then Katie made an inspection tour this morning and told me if you came back and saw the havoc I'd wreaked, you'd never set foot in the place again." He locked his arms around her waist. "That's not true, is it?"

Even though their reunion upstairs had been thoroughly satisfying, Lindsay reacted to his nearness with a tingling new desire to replay her homecoming. "How can I tell," she murmured, "when all the havoc has been cleared away? Did Katie do that?"

"I did it—solely in your honor." He slowly moved his lips from her forehead to the tip of her nose, dropping delicious little kisses along the way. "I slaved until nearly train time."

"You said you went to Hartford to make a wine delivery. Meeting the train, I was given to understand, was only incidental."

"Surely you didn't fall for that old story, did you?"

Sighing, she nestled closer against him. "The flowers are beautiful, Steven. But what if I hadn't come back tonight?"

"I suppose they could have hung on for a few more days." He put his finger under her chin and tilted her head back to pour the blue intensity of his eyes into hers. "But I'm not sure that I could have."

She teased shakily, "Because I'm so charming in bed?"

"Because you're so charming, period." His

voice hoarsened. "You winsome wench, I suppose you know you've spoiled me forever for any other woman."

Lindsay found it hard to breathe. "That's the nicest thing you've ever said to me, Mr. Strake."

"I have a whole list of nice things to say. I've been thinking them up for days. Come upstairs with me, and I'll lock the bedroom door and tell you what they are."

"We just came down from there."

"Oh, yes. So we did." He gave an exaggerated sigh and slid his hands down along her body, praising every curve before he reluctantly took his hands away. "I guess all that's left to us, then, is an omelet." Assuming a new briskness, he turned her toward the stove. "Will you do the honors?"

A misty smile curled Lindsay's lips. "Steven Strake, are you shy? Have I missed discovering that before?"

He said airily, "What makes you think you've discovered it now?"

"I think you were about to tell me something. And then you backed away."

"I haven't moved an inch."

The hammering of Lindsay's heart insisted that he had been on the brink of telling her at last that he loved her. "Weren't you poised to make a confession?"

"You mean disclosing my list of nice things?" With maddening indifference, he tweaked her cheek. "I think I'll save that for a time when we're not quite so hungry."

"Steven—" They were too close to resolving a crucial barrier, she felt, to let the moment go. "Doesn't the fact that we missed each other so terribly suggest something?"

"Yes, it does." He began making a great clatter as he searched for the omelet pan in the pot drawer. "It suggests that the next time you decide to leave, I'd better go with you."

"Really, Steven?" Lindsay was thrilled almost to speechlessness. She had a quick recollection of the loft in Soho with African violets blooming on the windowsills. "Would you really go with me?"

"Absolutely." He found the pan and set it down with a bang on the stove top. "Providing, of course, that your destination was the Bay of Fundy at incoming tide. Or a nice tennis and tiddlywinks weekend in the Poconos."

"Oh, *Steven*!" Tears of frustration stung at her eyelids. "When will you ever be serious?"

He turned around and for an instant an inscrutable look of longing stood in his eyes. But he quickly chased it away with a benign smile. "I'm serious now. I'm bordering on pernicious anemia. Feed me, lady."

THE NEXT several weeks went by swiftly. Whenever Lindsay thought of what might be happening with her songs in New York, time seemed to drag. But when she looked at the calendar, she saw that the days were leapfrogging toward Christmas. She racked her brain to think of something to give Steven. Cuff links? A watch? But nothing she came up with seemed special enough. Finally she decided to trust to luck that she would think of something before the twenty-fifth.

What occupied more of her thoughts each day was the closeness she and Steven had shared since her return from New York. He had been tender and caring before, but there was a new depth in his attentiveness. She saw how hard he had to work not to touch her every minute he was near her. When they were alone, he displayed a new kind of possessiveness that made him call out from the study door when she was in the kitchen, just to make sure she was still in the house. When she was at the piano he brought his law books down and sat in the armchair while she worked on the songs that now seemed to pour forth from her at a rate she could hardly keep up with. Frequently he took her into Terrapin Falls to spend evenings with friends he had never introduced her to before.

All of these things helped to ease Lindsay's anxiety about the future. Steven, she decided, was a man who pondered long over the changes he made in his life. She knew what a racking ordeal it had been for him to leave Dexter, Brink and Dexter, and now another decision just as traumatic was facing him.

Lindsay smiled to herself, walking down to her cottage one crisp afternoon. Whether Steven was quite prepared for it or not, they were going to get married. He might not know yet that separate lives for the two of them were out of the question now, but everything he did these days indicated that he loved her as deeply as she loved him. Eventually he would have to say so. And then they could begin making plans.

Actually, she thought with no small amount of pleasure, Steven might already be quietly making plans on his own. Three times recently she had seen letters on his desk from Dexter, Brink and Dexter. An increasing amount of his free time was spent poring over the law, while the wine books on the dining-room table gathered dust.

When she teased him about neglecting his role as vigneron, he only laughed and said he had memorized the contents of those books long before she had appeared on the scene. But he had admitted, under her persistent questioning, that he had entered into a correspondence with his old law firm. When her face lit up like a Roman candle at that news, he reminded her brusquely that a correspondence was not the same thing as practicing. She had nodded agreeably, but she had another reason to believe that operating the vineyard was no longer his prime concern. He had turned more responsibility over to Rachel, and that was a move that brought joy to her heart. It fit so nicely into her plans! She hoped he would never give up the winery entirely, but when they moved to New York. . . .

Suddenly she came face to face with Steven in the middle of the path. It was the first time she had seen him all day, and she lifted her lips eagerly for his kiss. "Where have you been hiding? Just because there were only menial tasks to do at the barn for a change, you needn't have played the recluse."

He turned around and swung into step beside her. "I had a project of my own to get out of the way," he told her. "But now it's in the mail, so I'm free as a bird."

In the mail. A letter to the law firm accepting their latest offer? Lindsay felt like dancing.

He said, "I've just come from your cottage." Sometimes he went snooping in her kitchen when his sweet tooth was on a rampage. But this time he said, "It's the drabbest place I've ever seen."

"What do you mean?" Up to now he had thoroughly approved of every personal touch she had added to the cottage. "I thought you liked the way I've arranged things."

"Generally speaking, yes." He assumed a lofty air. "But this is the Christmas season, Scrooge. And there's not so much as a holly berry in your house."

"In yours either!" she came back indignantly.

He wrapped an arm around her waist. "I know, and I think it's time we did something about that."

She loved it when he put his arms around her. His commanding strength close to her stirred up all kinds of lovely sensations. "What do you have in mind, sir?"

"I own a meadow up by Rappahannock Pond where I've never taken you. In summer, wild roses bloom there, along with wood orchids and oceans of Queen Anne's lace." He gazed down at her. "But this time of year, the main attraction is Christmas trees."

"Do you mean we're going to go there and cut our own tree?" Excitement bubbled out of her. "I haven't done that for years!"

"Because you've been off in the city," he chided mildly. "State your preference. Balsam or fir."

But she wouldn't be pinned down. "I have to look at every single tree growing in your meadow before I'll tell you that."

He groaned. "Come along then. Let's get started."

12

GATHERING the Christmas greenery took all afternoon. The meadow on Rappahannock Pond went up a hillside where more than evergreens grew. After Steven had cut down the tree they decided upon—a spicy balsam that Lindsay kept circling around to take whiffs of—they tramped up to the top of the hill and then made their way down slowly, cutting boughs of fir for the mantels in both houses and sprigs of berries for binding into the grapevine wreaths Lindsay planned to make that evening.

"I wish there were snow," she said once, gazing wistfully over the burnt-orange grass that still covered the ground.

"There will be," Steven promised. "A foot by Christmas at least."

Lindsay stared up at the cloudless sky. "There's no sign of it yet."

Steven chuckled. "In another week or so you'll be wondering when it will stop."

They went home then, with the Old Gray Mare looking like a moving forest. After dinner they popped corn and strung cranberries on the boughs of their tree. On the way home from the meadow, Lindsay had made Steven stop in Terrapin Falls for green and red paper, and after the other decorations were hung, she sat on the floor beneath the tree, pasting into festive window chains the strips Steven cut from it.

"My grandmother taught me how to make those," she said proudly when she finished draping the chains along the tops of the home-spun curtains. "Don't they add just the right touch to our old-fashioned decorations?"

Steven grinned. "I pronounce your Christmas preparations perfect."

"Our preparations," she corrected, planting a kiss squarely on his lips. "I think we have the most beautiful tree in the world."

"Now what?" Steven glanced at the pile of dried vines she had asked him to bring in from behind the barn where they were stacked for burning. "Is your wreath the next project?"

Lindsay let out a long sigh. "I can't get to that tonight. I'm all worn out with celebrating."

"Then come sit down on the sofa. I have something for you."

Lindsay's eyes widened. "What?"

"A present."

"It's not Christmas yet."

"This can't wait."

"What is it?" she called after him as eagerly

as a child. But watching him mount the stairs, she dared to wonder if it was a ring.

Her heart was pounding wildly when he came down again, but the box he was carrying was a wooden case large enough to hold a pair of shoes.

Lindsay did her best to hide her disappointment, but her crushed hopes made her ache. However, when Steven was seated beside her, and she raised the lid of the box, what she saw inside filled her with delight.

"Why, it's a crèche!" Excitement made her fingers tremble as she began drawing out the little wooden figures—the Christ child in the manger first, with every detail exquisitely carved. Then the shepherds and the patient wise men. Lambs and cows, the Madonna and Joseph.

When they were all arranged in front of her, Lindsay's smoky eyes glowed with appreciation of Steven's generosity. "The uncle who made the furniture carved these, didn't he?"

Steven nodded. "They were his last gift to my mother. They're for your mantel." His strangely penetrating look quickened her pulse. "And to keep afterward if you like."

To commemorate for the rest of our lives our first Christmas together? But she bit back the words. Her disappointment of a few minutes before had graphically reminded her that only in her own heart was anything settled between them.

She breathed out softly, "I'll treasure them

always." She meant it, but the ache in her breast made her wonder how she could bear to look at them next year if Steven were not at her side.

THE CALL Lindsay was expecting from Jonathon came the next evening. She was in her cottage sitting on the sofa, admiring the crèche on the mantel and the boughs of fir on each side while she waited for Steven to come and spend the next few hours with her. When he had walked her home the evening before he had brought the grapevines with him and now they were all in a heap in a corner of the room, waiting for the two of them to make an ambitious half a dozen wreaths for gifts to the winery crew.

She heard Steven's knock, but before she could get to the door, he flung it open.

"Jonathon Page is on the phone," he told her.

Lindsay took time only to grab a sweater, and then she raced ahead of Steven up the path. She hardly had breath enough to say hello when she reached the phone in the farmhouse kitchen. But Jonathon did most of the talking anyway.

During the long one-sided conversation, Steven leaned against the sink and scowled impatiently each time she said, "Yes! Yes, I see! Go on!"

But finally she hung up and went flying into

his arms. "They're doing the show in a really good off-Broadway theater! They're using my songs! The contracts are ready to be signed!"

"Wait a minute. Slow down." But Steven's irritation had vanished. He laughed and held her close. "Start at the first and tell me all about it."

They went into the parlor with Lindsay babbling all the way. The young producer had secured the backers... Jonathon had promised him eight more songs... they hoped to go into production by Easter.

Steven listened intently to everything that spilled out of her. Finally, he said, "That means you'll be going to New York right away."

"Tomorrow, to sign the contracts, and to work out the details with Jonathon for the new music." She hesitated. "Did I tell you? He's coming for me." She saw the frown forming on Steven's brow and hurried on. "He suggested that we could talk on the drive back. But it shouldn't take longer than a few days to go over everything with the producer. I'll finish up my last-minute shopping—" She still had to find the perfect gift for Steven. "And then I'll be back here."

"For how long?"

The unexpected bluntness of his inquiry brought her up short. *That depends on you,* she wanted to retort. But pride kept her from it. He still hadn't shared with her any of the arrangements he was obviously making with his old law firm. She could only assume that in time he would, but until then, for whatever reasons he had, he had chosen to keep her in limbo—about that, as well as about everything else that concerned their future.

She answered tartly, "I'll have to see how things go in New York."

Her parents weren't coming for Christmas, though Steven had called and invited them himself. It would be just the two of them, Steven and herself. It would be perfect if only there wasn't this communications barrier between them. She dared not think it was anything else. If only they could make some definite plans before the demands of the show closed in on her.

Suddenly she became aware of Steven's brooding gaze, and a rush of love welled up inside of her. How difficult it must be for him to think of uprooting himself, of going back to the city he despised. But his career—and hers too—was too specialized for them to live anywhere else. If she expected her music to go anywhere, she had to be where musical events were taking place; she had to keep her finger on the pulse of what was happening on Broadway; she needed the glitter and the glamour of big city life to stimulate her creative juices. And Steven was a corporation lawyer. There weren't many corporations in Terrapin Falls!

But apparently the idea of leaving was weighing heavily upon him. Probably it hadn't helped tonight to have to face up to the fact that shortly she would be leaving, too. She felt a stir of excitement, realizing that they had almost reached the point where they could no longer pretend that today was all that mattered. Still, her heart went out to him. The farm and the Connecticut countryside were rooted deep in his soul ... as they were in hers. Had he forgotten that?

Kneeling in front of his chair, she said softly, "Steven, I love the city. I won't deny that. I love the way it makes me feel about myself, as if I'm charged with a special kind of electricity. But the farm—" she raised her smoky eyes, smoldering with love "—the farm will always come first with me. No matter what happens in New York this time, I'll be home for Christmas. Wild horses couldn't keep me away."

He put out his hand and smoothed her shining hair. "Home," he said huskily. "I'll be waiting for you with all the candles burning."

For a while longer they sat talking. Lindsay's exuberance came back. Wouldn't Jonathon be surprised, she said to Steven, when he discovered that she had written half a dozen more songs, some of which she was sure could be worked into companion pieces for those they had already submitted to the producer?

In front of the fire, she clasped her hands together gleefully. "Really, most of the hard work is done!"

Then suddenly her eyes opened wide. "Oh— my goodness!"

Steven sat forward. "What is it?"

"I've forgotten something terribly important!" She got to her feet and raced out to the kitchen. "I have to tell Katie."

Steven came after her, reaching her just as she put out her hand for the telephone. "Wait a minute. Does Katie have to know tonight? Just for this evening can't we have a private celebration?"

Lindsay wanted that, too. She kissed him quickly. But she was bent on contacting Katie first. "I have some fabulous news for her that can't keep. I don't know how I could have forgotten to mention it, except that everything else that's happened this evening is so fabulous, too." She ran her hands up along his shoulders, noticing with a shiver of erotic pleasure their sturdy resistance to her caress.

"Katie," she announced in husky triumph, "is going to audition for our show."

"What?" Steven stared.

"I know—" She laughed, sympathizing with his look of astonishment. "Imagine what *her* reaction will be when she hears the news! It's too fantastic, isn't it? But the audition is set up for four o'clock on Thursday. So Katie will have to ride in with us tomorrow."

She reached again for the telephone, but

once more Steven stopped her, less gently this time. "Jonathon has arranged for Katie to audition in New York?"

Lindsay frowned at Steven's hand clamped around her wrist. "It wasn't entirely Jonathon's doing. I suggested it, of course. Jonathon has never heard Katie sing."

"Lindsay—" He released her, but there was no mistaking now that he was angry. "Katie is talented. But she'll never be a Broadway star."

"How do you know?" Lindsay's own temper flared. "She has a marvelous range. And I can tell you this—she's much too good to sit around Terrapin Falls, singing in the church choir for the rest of her days."

Steven said coldly, "I suppose you're the ultimate judge of what she ought to do with her life."

Lindsay's face flooded with color. "What kind of crack is that? All I've done is put in a good word for her. And it's only a bit part, for heaven's sake!" She glared at Steven, trying to imagine why he was so upset. "But even if she were offered a lead role, why should you object?"

Steven's strong chin jutted. "I object because you and Jonathon Page are playing God."

Lindsay gasped. "Have you lost your mind?"

"I think you have. If you believe your own destiny lies in New York, that's your business. You're a mature woman entitled to make whatever decisions you want. But Katie is only a child. You and your friend Jonathon are yanking up a perfectly content small-town girl and throwing her to the wolves."

Lindsay choked back a laugh that was half a sob. "If you could see yourself! Who's playing God now?" She flung his own accusation back at him. "Are you the ultimate judge? The honorable Steven Strake, without whom it would be impossible to separate the wolves from the lambs? Let me tell you something, your honor! Katie is not a child, and she is not going to be content forever pasting labels on your wine bottles and ramming corks into their necks. She has a marvelous talent that's going to waste here."

Steven's lip curled. "So now her Fairy Godmother has finally come to her rescue."

"It's my privilege to rescue her—and it's my duty! She deserves a chance to develop her voice. And I'm going to do everything in my power to see that she gets it, no matter what you think."

"Or no matter what happens to her?" The glacier blue of Steven's eyes bored into Lindsay. "So what if she does get a bit part in a New York show? Where does she go when it's over? What if it closes after one night?"

Lindsay's eyes flashed. "Then she can come back home, and your opinion will be vindicated. Is that what you're thinking?"

"I'm thinking that she'll be ruined for Terrapin Falls because she'll consider herself a star. She won't be content here, and she won't belong in New York. That's the happy future you've blocked out for her."

"I know what's the matter with you," Lindsay raged. "It's your precious winery, isn't it? It's Christmas time, your big season, and the only two members of your staff who can crawl into your tanks are deserting the ship. Why don't you go out, Steven, and hire some child labor? Train a couple of kids to scrape your tartrates and then lock them up at night so they won't find out there's a world outside that might offer them a more fulfilling life."

Steven clamped his teeth together and whirled away toward the parlor. Lindsay ran after him. "You can't deny the selfishness of your motives, can you?"

But her heart was pounding. The accusations she had hurled at him had left a bitter taste in her mouth.

Steven spun around. The firelight behind him outlined his powerful body, tensed like a lion's. Through the tears that glazed her eyes, Lindsay could see on the piano the pink cyclamen that had refused to stop blooming even after all the other flowers Steven had bought for her had died.

He struck out at her harshly. "'The farm will always come first with me.' Isn't that what you said?"

"Steven—" Her voice caught. "I meant that!"

"That's hard to believe when you're sneering at what goes on here. All your talk about loving it here, loving the routine, the work you do at the winery. I don't think you've meant anything you've said since you came here."

"You know that's not so!"

"I didn't ask you to come here, you know. And I've said from the start that you're free to go whenever you choose."

She blanched at his words, "But Katie isn't free. Why is that, Steven?"

"Katie is a child."

"And you think two adults are leading her astray! How ridiculous. You're letting a blind, personal prejudice get in the way of good judgment. Katie is nineteen years old now. She knows what she wants. She has the right to try to achieve it."

"Have you spoken to her parents? Do you know what their views are?"

"Of course I don't know! That's Katie's problem. If they object, she'll have to work it out. All I can do is offer her a chance for success. And all you can do, if you treat her fairly, is to give her your good wishes. Steven—" Suddenly she was pleading. "Forget about Katie for a minute. We aren't really quarreling about her anyway, are we?"

She laid trembling hands flat against his chest and felt beneath her palms that his heart was pounding, too. "Oh, Steven, you're wrong when you say I haven't loved it here. These past few months have been the best months of my life. They've given me a new perspective, the courage to make a fresh start. Every hour I've spent at the winery, every precious moment I've shared with you, I'll cherish always. But you must have known that music is central to my life . . . the way the law once was for you—"

He broke in curtly, "Your career is your own. I've always said that."

"Yes—but haven't you only been paying it lip service? You're resisting the fact that I have to go where my career calls me!"

"Do you have to, Lindsay?" His gaze pierced her. "Do you really?"

"No, of course not," she choked back. "Not if you know of someone who's producing musicals in Terrapin Falls!"

He set his jaw and started to turn away, but Lindsay held on to him. "Do you think I can't understand how you might have become disillusioned with a city practice? I can see what living in the country means to you. I can sympathize with your fascination for winemaking. It fascinates me, too. But I can also see that you're still drawn irresistibly to the law, that it still absorbs you as nothing else does. Why do you find that so hard to admit? Oh, Steven, darling—" She took hold of his shoulders. "For both our sakes, can't you pick up where you left off with good grace and stop playing at life?"

"Playing!" he broke in explosively. "Is that what you think I've been doing?"

"Lots of people do it. My parents are a prime example, people who settled for a pleasant, easy existence rather than face the challenge of fully exploring their potential."

White with fury, Steven shook himself free. "Why, you self-righteous little prig!" His voice whipped at her. "Do you think your view of exploring potential is the only view? What qualifies you to pass judgment on how your parents spend their days? What do you know about the challenge I find in making fine wines? Or what I've learned lying in a meadow studying the stars? I was never disillusioned with the law," he snapped. "I was disillusioned with the petty little people who think New York is the center of the universe. I was disillusioned with thieves who club you in the subway, and with trash on the streets, and the stupidity of spending half my life on commuter trains."

He gave her a pitying look. "But if that's what appeals to you, you're welcome to it. And so is Katie—if she's fool enough to go with you."

Lindsay's eyes blazed, "If it's such a terrible place, why are you making plans to go back to it?"

Steven snorted. "You're a dreamer if you think I am."

She caught her breath suddenly. "But what about Dexter, Brink—?" Her eyes raced across his face. "You're corresponding with them!"

"Because I've agreed to research their briefs for them." He glared at her. "But I don't have to sit in their laps to do it."

Her face crumpled suddenly. "I thought—"

"I know what you thought—that if you kept after me long enough, you'd wear down my resistance."

Her temper blazed again. "I only hoped you'd give up your stubbornness. But I would never have insisted that you return to New York against your will."

His jaw jutted. "And I have never insisted that you stay here against yours."

Tears were streaming down her face, but pride drew her erect. "Then I guess it's a good thing Jonathon is coming for me tomorrow."

"I guess it is," he said stonily.

Their glances locked.

"I've changed my mind." Her voice quavered. "When I leave tomorrow, I won't be coming back."

"What you do is entirely up to you."

A fresh surge of rage almost choked her. "I am so sick of the pompous way you say that!"

He turned away. "Then that's another reason for you to be glad you're leaving."

She raised her voice in a shrill taunt that carried after him into the hallway. "Do you mind if I telephone Katie now?"

His icy retort came back over his shoulder. "Talk all night if you want to."

The door slammed while she was dialing.

13

LINDSAY finished her conversation with an ecstatic Katie as quickly as she could and then hurried down the hill toward her cottage. It had taken her only a few minutes after Steven slammed out to realize how senseless their quarrel had been. Jonathon's call had precipitated it. It had caught them both off guard, unready to make the decisions they had postponed so long. Defensively they had lashed out at each other.

Steven also must have realized all that by now. As she walked, she glanced around, expecting that any moment he would step out on the path and apologize. She had apologies to make, too.

Much of what she had said to Steven she was willing to stick by. But he had never been pompous. And he was right to have called her a self-righteous prig for criticizing her parents. At the root of her attitude, she realized guiltily, was the feeling that they had deserted her. A childish idea, if there ever was one, since she had moved to California first, leaving them behind. Besides that, they had explored their potential years ago. In their retirement years they deserved to spend their leisure any way they wanted.

She drew near the cottage, imagining that Steven was waiting inside. Smiling, she pictured him abject before the fire. But when she flung open the door, only the dying embers of the blaze she had started earlier greeted her. Everything else was just as she left it when she rushed out to answer Jonathon's call. The pile of grapevines waited to be wound into wreaths, the fir boughs on the mantel gave off their Christmasy fragrance.

Suddenly the enormity of what had happened burst upon her. A senseless quarrel? Who was she kidding? Her breath caught in a sob and she sank down on the quaint little sofa. Steven had no intention of marrying her . . . he wasn't going to New York . . . and she was leaving forever.

For weeks she had longed to discuss the future. Now they had. And everything was over.

A storm of weeping shook her. Once the door rattled and she raised her tear-swollen face. But it was only the wind knocking, and she cried again for her broken dreams . . . for the times she had lain in Steven's arms . . . and for the times she never would again.

Outside the moon sailed across the clear Connecticut sky. At last she roused herself and gazed woodenly around at the cottage she had adored. There were a great many things that needed doing before she left the next morning.

Numbly she began packing, first a small bag with the things she would need immediately, and then everything else. Out of a tiny storeroom off the kitchen, she brought out the cardboard boxes that had arrived with her in September, and slowly she went about divesting each room of her personal possessions . . . the wineglasses she and Steven had drunk from . . . his favorite sofa pillow. She left undisturbed only the crèche, which she couldn't bear to touch.

Then in a furious surge of frustration she cleaned the cottage from top to bottom, dusting every inch of it and polishing each piece of the beloved furniture until everything shone.

By sunup the whole place was sparkling. Exhausted, Lindsay bathed and then wrapped a robe around her. Over a cup of coffee she gazed into the dusky quiet of the parlor.

Who would live here next? The thought of anyone taking her place brought tears to her eyes. Maybe Steven would feel so bitterly toward her that he would lock the door and throw the key away.

Then she heard his knock. This time there was no mistaking it. Firm and assertive, it sounded again. And who else would come at dawn!

He was freshly shaven, she saw when she opened the door, but he looked as weary as she herself felt. Devouring him eagerly with her gaze, she was aware that all of her senses were clamoring for his touch. The scent of his shaving lotion assaulted her nostrils, bringing back a thousand memories. Her fingers ached to smooth away the creases around his eyes. Only their unresolved quarrel enabled her to keep her hands clasped tightly in front of her.

Steven spoke first. "Did I wake you?"

That he would ask tore at her heart. Who knew better than he how she looked waking up ... pink-cheeked and fresh ... eager for his kiss? Nothing at all like the way she looked now. One of her hands moved to the collar of her robe. Probably he had guessed, too, in that piercing way he was regarding her, that beneath the silk cloth she wore no clothes.

Embarrassed that she longed for him to remove even that, she said stiffly, "I've been up all night packing."

"You needn't have cleaned the house." His gaze went past her to the spotless rooms from which all the personal touches of her stay had been removed except for the Christmas decorations that seemed a mockery now. "I planned to have someone come in and do it."

"I wasn't able to sleep."

They stared at each other for a long awkward moment. To Lindsay it seemed that Steven was reaching out for her in the same way she was yearning for him. His gaze softened, but he made no move to touch her.

Then abruptly he held out a check. "I brought this. For your shopping."

It had always been a joke between them that what he paid her for working a month in the winery was less than she had earned for the background music of one commercial in California. But now she saw that what he was offering her was twice what she normally made. She glanced up, ready to protest. If he thought he could buy her off—

But he said before she could speak, "Everyone is getting a Christmas bonus. We had a good year."

A vintage year. Tears stung at her eyelids. *Begun too late, over too soon.* She folded the check away in the pocket of her robe. Then suddenly she saw he was about to walk away. "Do you want to come in? I have a fresh pot of coffee."

He hesitated, and she darted away toward the kitchen. When she came back into the parlor, he was standing in front of the fireplace, looking around the empty room. "When do you expect Jonathon?"

The bleakness of his tone made her heart leap. "I'm not sure."

"I suppose Katie was thrilled with your news."

"Yes. She was thrilled." A desperate sense of urgency came over Lindsay. They were discussing trivialities and the world was about to come to an end! She took a step forward. "Steven—"

At the same moment he moved toward her, her name on his lips. They halted in front of each other. For an instant it seemed that time had rolled back... there had been no quarrel... no angry words.

Then Steven jammed his hands into his pockets and turned away. "You were about to say—?"

She looked at his chiseled profile and tightly compressed lips and swallowed her words. Clearly it was too late to tell him that she loved him. Even if she had found him last night it would have been too late. The world had already ended and they were standing in the ashes. She choked out, "I wanted you to know that as soon as I'm settled I'll send for my things. I'll leave the key to the cottage with Rachel."

"There's no need to bother Rachel." He paused and cleared his throat. "Later this afternoon, I'll come back and lock up."

An endless silence stretched out between them.

"Why aren't you taking the crèche?" he said.

"I couldn't." Her nails bit into the palms of her hands. "Not now."

Suddenly he spun around, his face a granite mask. "You do understand, don't you, Lindsay, that there's no way I could ever live in New York again?"

She pulled in her breath. "Yes, I understand."

"I'm sorry if you thought I could." His gaze burned into her. "I tried to make it clear from the start that this is my home now, that it always will be."

"You did." Her voice fell to a whisper. "You made it very clear"

"You have to understand, too, that it doesn't matter what we said to each other last night. If you ever want to come back here—"

She cut him off, lifting her trembling chin. "Are you offering me a haven because you don't think I'll make it in New York?"

"If anyone can make it, you will."

All at once she said in a gasp, "You're just going to let me go, aren't you?"

"Yes—" But he moved suddenly and took her in his arms, crushing her against his chest so that through the thin cloth of her robe, she felt the hard cage of his ribs and the long line of his thighs pressing into her.

"It's the way I feel about my music, isn't it?" A flood of tears soaked his chest. "You've pretended that you didn't mind, but all along you hated the part it plays in my life as much as Winston did."

He shook his head, moving his lips in her hair. "No, that's not true, Lindsay. It's never been true."

"You feel it would always stand between us the way it's doing now. And that's why you're letting me go."

"No."

She clung to him, weeping. "Then why are we saying goodbye, Steven?"

He took her gently by the shoulders and held her away from him. "Because you want to leave," he said quietly. "And I have to stay."

"It can't be as simple as that!"

"It isn't simple at all."

Hours of longing and frustration congealed suddenly into fresh fury. Disregarding all restraint, she blazed out at him. "It isn't true that you couldn't live again in New York! You could come with me, Steven! If you weren't so stubborn, so biased against the past!"

"And you could stay," he said flatly, dropping his arms.

Her damp smoky eyes flashed fire. "Why should I have to make all the sacrifices?"

His jaw tightened. "That's the point you've missed all along. I've never asked you to sacrifice anything."

"Then why did you come here this morning?" she stormed. "To torture me? To drag out my misery to the last bitter instant?"

"I came," he said, staring straight through her, "because in the middle of the night I reached out for you and you weren't there."

He walked quickly to the door. "Goodbye, Lindsay. If you ever need me, you'll know where I am."

I need you now! But if he couldn't tell her he loved her, nothing could make her say those words aloud.

The door closed with a click of finality.

For a moment she stood where he had left her, tears pouring down her face. Then she ran to one of the high front windows and climbed up on the calico-covered footstool for one last glimpse of him.

Stretching, she could see him halfway up the hill, the first rays of sun streaming across his back. Suddenly as she watched, a full-grown stag bounded out of the vineyard into his path. It halted when it saw Steven, its brown coat glistening with dew, plumes of steam issuing from its nostrils. Steven stopped so close to the deer, he could have touched it.

For a quivering instant neither moved. Then in a graceful arching leap, the stag cleared a row of grapevines and trotted off into the woods.

Lindsay clutched the windowsill, watching Steven finish his climb. The ache in her heart told her she had witnessed the kind of moment Steven lived for...a precious, crystal moment that he would remember long after he had forgotten her.

She sank down on the calico footstool and cried until she had no more tears.

14

A HEAVY SNOW FELL the first night Katie and Lindsay were in New York, and when they rose in the morning, the city had turned into a glittering fairyland.

"Look how gorgeous everything is!" Katie crowed, munching a breakfast roll as she leaned on the windowsill of the tiny furnished room they had temporarily rented together.

Dressing, Lindsay paused to watch the starry flakes swirl past. "It's lovely," she agreed. But her voice held only an echo of Katie's enthusiasm. On their small transistor radio, a weatherman was giving an account of the storm. Connecticut had languished on the fringes, he reported enviously. It was crisp and cold there, but still sunny.

Lindsay's gaze lost its focus as she pictured Steven striding off in the crackling air toward the winery. He would be wearing his mackinaw and his scuffed brown boots. He would be whistling. *Steven.* An ache of longing spread inside her. All night he had haunted her dreams...smiling...whispering...holding her close to his warmth. But when she woke with his name on her lips at some terrible dark hour, it was Katie who breathed at her side in the narrow bed. Lindsay clutched a pillow instead of Steven's wide shoulders and she soaked it with her tears.

Now, dressing to go to Jonathon's studio, her face felt puffy, her mind sluggish and uninterested in what the day might hold. She longed to return to her dreams, to Steven's arms. Knowing she could not, she found it difficult to hide her irritation at Katie's high spirits and effusive chatter as the girl darted around the room, trying on one outfit and then discarding it the next instant in favor of another one.

Finally Katie herself wearied and plopped down on the side of the bed to watch Lindsay pull on her panty hose. "Maybe I should just go out and buy myself something exotic, especially for the audition." She tipped her head inquiringly. "What do you think?"

"I think you'd be making a mistake." A knot formed in Lindsay's stomach. Away from the farm Katie suddenly seemed five years younger. A child, as Steven had insisted. Too inexperienced and impressionable to be thrown to the wolves. But it was too late to look back.

Lindsay said as calmly as she could, "Wear the simplest thing you have. You don't want your clothes to speak so loudly your voice can't be heard."

Katie sighed. "That's true. Oh, Lindsay—"

she gazed in fond admiration at her friend "—have I told you how grateful I am to you for giving me this chance?"

Lindsay smiled wryly. "Only half a dozen times an hour since we left Terrapin Falls." The knot in her stomach tightened. "But you'd better wait to see what happens," she warned. "Later you might not feel so grateful."

Katie's freckled face paled. "Does that mean you think I won't be chosen?"

"No, of course not." Smitten with all kinds of guilt, Lindsay hastened to reassure her. "You've a wonderful voice. I think you're a cinch for the part."

"Honestly?"

"Honestly. It's just that you have to remember that the New York stage is a far cry from the choir loft of the Congregational church. You have a big adjustment to make." Searching under the bed for her shoes, she thought of her own predicament. "There may be some lonely hours ahead."

"I can handle them," Katie replied jauntily.

Youth, Lindsay thought, suddenly feeling a hundred. But she said in a lighter tone as she got to her feet, "I'm sure you can. I just want to make certain you know that the next few months won't be all peaches and cream. For one thing, you'll have to get a job to tide you over until rehearsals begin the middle of January."

The straightforward smile Lindsay had liked

from the first day she met Katie now spread over her face. "Yes, mother dear."

Then the girl's expression softened. "But whatever else happens, you've made it possible for me to come this far. Even if I bomb out at the audition, at least I won't die a gray old granny without having had my moment in the sun. That's what I owe you, Lindsay. And I'll never forget it."

Lindsay's throat tightened. Leaning over, she gave Katie a fierce hug. "What's more important for you to remember is that confidence is half the game. When you get up on that stage this morning, don't think of anything except how good you are. Give them your best, Katie."

"You bet I will." Katie's eyes glistened. "I'll make you proud of me."

"You're too late. I already am."

They finished dressing, Lindsay in a more optimistic frame of mind and Katie as playful as a puppy, decking herself out in the simple skirt and quiet beige sweater Lindsay advised.

But when they were out on the street with only an hour standing between Katie and the audition, Lindsay sensed her nervousness.

"Come to Jonathon's with me," she suggested. "Then you'll know where we're working, and you can come back there when you're through and tell us how everything went."

"I know you're anxious to get on with your

own business—" Katie reached out suddenly and clutched her hand "—but could you possibly come with me?"

"To the rehearsal hall?" Lindsay hesitated. "Do you really want me to?"

"Oh, Lindsay—" Katie's teeth chattered "—I think I'll die if you don't."

WAITING IN A DARKENED BACK ROW of the theater for Katie's turn to sing, Lindsay wrestled with a new awareness of how impersonal the city could be. The director of the musical had been pleasant enough when she introduced herself as the composer for the production he was casting. But as a way of reminding her that he was in charge on this occasion, he had not invited her to sit with the privileged few who surrounded him. No one, Lindsay mused, cared at this moment what she was feeling. Or what Katie felt, either. It didn't matter to the director or to those hanging on his every word that a young girl's dreams were pinned on his decision. He had a job to do, and he knew Katie as a number only. Without a pang he could say no and crush her hopes forever.

Earlier, walking over to the theater with Katie, Lindsay had tried to be glad that winter had come at last. She loved the city when it was blanketed in white, she had told herself staunchly, but the cold bleak buildings towering over her and the unfamiliar faces surging by had made her doubt her reasons for wanting to return to this unfeeling metropolis.

Trudging along beside the nervous Katie, she had found herself yearning for the loving support of the team at the winery. She yearned for the quiet serenity of Steven's Rappahannock meadow instead of the snow that was stinging her cheeks... for the evergreens crowding the hillside and the burnt-orange grass. Even the pain of remembering that Steven had chosen the Connecticut countryside in preference to being with her failed to ease her longing.

She missed everything about her Connecticut experience, missed it so intensely that even the sound of her own melodies floating back from the theater's stage was overlaid in her mind with the clear piping whistle of orchard orioles and the pleasant lowing of Holsteins in the hilltop pasture across from the winery.

She felt starved suddenly for simple pleasures—sheets drying in the wind, an apple picked from the tree at the side of her cottage. The complex search for a place to stay the night before had helped her to understand Steven's point of view better. And understanding him, she missed him that much more.

Then, all at once she realized that the girl stepping into the spotlight was Katie. Lindsay caught her breath, her attention riveted on the forlorn figure standing alone, as fragile-appearing as a leaf in the wind on the wide stage.

But the next minute the powerful fluid range of Katie's soprano took over. A thrill of excitement swept through Lindsay as she realized that the song Katie had chosen was the one Steven's lovemaking had inspired. Lindsay's lips parted as nostalgia, sharp and bittersweet, gripped her. She recalled Steven standing glumly over her in the predawn light of the parlor, listening while she picked out the same six notes again and again. What a struggle B flat had given her! But this moment made it worth every second of her anguish.

Glancing around, she saw that Katie's audience was captivated. A boy sweeping the aisle had stopped to lean on his broom. Near the ceiling a pair of electricians on a scaffold paused to listen. And the director, transfixed by Katie's vibrant tones, stood beside the piano as tensely alert as an exclamation mark.

Then as the last throbbing notes died away there was utter silence, a suspension of breath almost, and then thunderous applause.

Lindsay got to her feet, tears shining in her eyes. Now she knew why she was here. This was what she was born for—to write songs other people would clamor to sing and to hear. She could no more deny that creative part of herself than a bird could refuse to fly, no matter how much she loved Steven. Leaving him was a wrench she doubted she'd ever recover from. He was her heart, her soul. But listening to Katie, she was sure at last that she had made the only possible decision. New York was where she belonged.

FOR THE REST OF THE MORNING Lindsay floated blissfully on Katie's triumph. Over lunch with Jonathon she was still reliving the audition.

"When Katie finished singing, Jonathon, that was it! The director told the other girls they might as well go home. Katie won without even a contest."

"Of course. What did you expect?" But Jonathon's tone clearly implied that all he cared about was the score, not who would sing it.

"Besides that," Lindsay went on, disregarding his lack of interest, "she's found a job—at a little wine-and-cheese shop a block down from where we're staying. They hired her in a minute when they learned she had worked in a winery."

"I agree that Connecticut Katie is a winner," Jonathon commented dryly. "But what you and I need to concentrate on, my dear, is songs, not protégées."

"I *have* songs." Lindsay opened her purse with a flourish, prepared to hand over the six she had brought with her from the farm. But a sudden intuitive warning made her hold back all but two of them. "Here—" She passed them across the table. "Have a look at these."

Jonathon took his time studying the notes

she had written. Finally he looked up with un-
mistakable admiration glittering in his eyes.
"Darling, you're a gold mine."

"Of course. What did you expect?" It pleased
her to speak in the same bored tone he had
used on her. But in the long interval while she
had waited for his approval, the euphoria that
had buoyed her all morning abruptly de-
parted. All at once she felt as drained and de-
pressed as when she woke up holding a pillow
instead of Steven's wide shoulders.

She glanced distractedly around the restaurant. Annabelle's in Hartford had more charm
than this place, she concluded. The wine
she'd had with her lunch seemed brackish
and insipid compared to the Strake Farm
Rieslings she had grown used to. And Jonathon's compliments, she thought in despair,
had no power to chase away the memories of
blond granite-jawed Steven that had stalked
her all day.

Fighting an urge to weep, she picked up her
purse. "Do you mind if we go?"

"What's your hurry?" Jonathon eyed her
curiously. "I thought I might have another cup
of coffee."

"If I make a cup for you at the loft, won't
that do as well?"

"You're on edge." He cocked his head. "Why?"

"I didn't sleep well."

"Tension," Jonathon diagnosed. "You'll have
to sign up for an exercise class at the Y." He

gave her a complacent smile and hailed a waiter. "It's hard work being half of a famous team, you know."

Lindsay answered sharply, "We aren't famous yet."

"Ah—but we will be." He leaned back to light an expensive cigar. "If not from this show, then from the next one. Or the one after that."

Noting Lindsay's nervous pinched look, he picked up her hand from the table and squeezed it. "Relax, sweetheart. There's nothing to worry about. You and I are an unbeatable combination."

AN UNBEATABLE COMBINATION, Lindsay kept reminding herself as the weekend passed. Jonathon Page and Lindsay Hancock would be the toast of the New York stage, she told the mirror as she dressed. Already a notice had appeared in *Variety*, hinting at a super success that a vibrant new twosome was putting together off Broadway. Each time she met with the producer, he was more enthusiastic about her talent.

"The only trouble is," Lindsay confided nervously to Katie late one night at the start of the new week, "I seem to have dried up."

Gazing at Lindsay's ripe form stretched out on the bed in a pale apricot nightgown, Katie laughed. "Yeah, I can see that you have—like a hundred-year-old prune."

"It's my music I'm talking about!" Lindsay said sharply. "Since I came to New York, I haven't composed a single new song."

"Well, my goodness," Katie exclaimed, "you've hardly had time."

But Lindsay knew time wasn't her problem. She was deadlocked and for no reason she could explain. At the farm, bright new melodies had swarmed daily in her head. She'd hardly had time to write them down before new ones were flocking in her brain. Now when she was at Jonathon's piano, the only rhythm she could depend on was the slow sullen beat of her heart. "I'm feeling hemmed in, Katie," she explained unwillingly. "Panicky, really."

Katie sat down on the bed, her eyes full of sympathy. "Does Jonathon know?"

Lindsay shook her head. "He hasn't guessed because I'm feeding him a backlog I composed at the winery."

"How big a backlog? Enough to see you through this show?"

"I think so." There was the finale, of course, but if worse came to worst, she might get away with arranging a medley of the other songs.

Katie released a sigh of relief. "Then what are you worrying about?"

"I'm worrying," Lindsay fretted, "because on the farm, music came to me from every direction. But here in New York, at the 'center of the universe,'" she quoted Steven bleakly, "the squeaking chains on the park swings are making more music than I am."

"Don't be so concerned. It's only a temporary block. One of those adjustments you warned me about."

"Maybe so." But what Lindsay feared, what she was too desolate even to think about, was that she had left all her songs behind in the long peaceful evenings in Steven's parlor ... in the golden afternoons of autumn when she had lain in the sweet-smelling grass of the woods with Steven at her side. ...

Always before, New York had given her an electrical charge. It was an irresistible stimulant to her creative juices. Now all she felt was a dull throbbing current of misery. The glitter and excitement that was supposed to vitalize her had so far produced only a numbing effect.

She let out a shivering sigh. "Maybe I've become allergic to the city."

Katie nodded solemnly. "I can see that New York might get on your nerves after the quiet of the country. All the traffic, you know, and the noise."

But it was plain to Lindsay that Katie was thriving on everything the city had to offer. Every morning she went to work singing Lindsay's praises for having opened the golden door for her, and every evening she went out with new friends to explore New York's sparkling nightlife. She had made enough plans with her new cronies to keep her busy for at least six months.

And I, Lindsay thought dejectedly, *am homesick!*

Katie eyed her glum countenance thoughtfully. "Maybe," she said hesitantly, "you can't write music because you're missing Steven. I haven't wanted to pry, but I know you haven't heard from him." She wrinkled her freckled brow. "Did you quarrel?"

"No." Lindsay turned over on her side, hoping her view of the garish wallpaper that dwarfed the room would blot out Steven's accusing face. "We had a minor disagreement about an unimportant matter. It certainly has nothing to do with this."

"Are you sure, Lindsay?"

"I've told you before," Lindsay snapped, "we're only friends."

Katie lay down and pulled up the covers. "I know that's what you said. But if you're having trouble composing—"

Lindsay cut her off. "You haven't found it necessary to be in love to sing a love song, have you?" She shut off the light with a decisive click. "Why should you assume that *I* have to be in love to write one?"

THE WEEK WORE ON, but nothing in Lindsay's situation improved. Confessing her distress to Katie had only made her more acutely aware of it. And Jonathon certainly did nothing to help.

"You seem to think I'm a faucet you can turn on and songs will pour out," she told him irritably one afternoon just before Christmas.

"And why not?" He turned around from his desk to stare at her, slumped over the piano. "You've given me a fistful of great ones in less than a week. This last one is a dandy, too." He crossed his arms over his chest. "But we do desperately need the finale. When are you going to come up with that?"

"Tracey said I could have a month to work on it."

"Producers make promises like that. Then they wake you up in the middle of the night and want three stanzas and a chorus before breakfast."

"I told you I'd have it, Jonathon. Just leave me alone."

He quirked an eyebrow. "I hope you're not brooding about that wine maker."

"You know what his name is. Don't be rude. And for your information, I'm not brooding about anything."

But she could see from Jonathon's skeptical look that he had guessed that Steven was always on her mind. She couldn't pass a blond man on the street without emotionally tying herself in knots. She hated the telephone because it rang only for Katie.

What made it all worse was the frustrating

fickleness of her talent. While married to Winston, she had confidently blamed domestic unrest for her failure to create. Winston was always after her to be doing something else. But in Connecticut, where there were constant demands of all kinds, music had always been at her fingertips.

How was it, she wondered bitterly, that she could compose while gasping for breath in a stainless-steel tank, and here in Jonathon's spacious loft where her only job was to write music, not a single original measure presented itself?

The past tortuous week had made her conscious of something else, too. The theory she had always held to, that she had to drop everything else and set down a score the minute it occured to her, had never applied at the winery. Except for the first song she had written that had made her leave Steven's bed before dawn, she had scratched notes down as best she could between chores, and the songs she turned out so haphazardly were the hits Jonathon and Tracey were praising now. Crushing grapes or scraping tartrates, she had somehow managed to carry the melodies in her head and benefited from doing so.

"What are you scowling at?" Jonathon chided. "That keyboard is the best friend you have."

Lindsay rose abruptly from the piano bench. "I'm going for a walk."

He commented dryly, "An excellent idea. You're giving me the jitters. And while you're out, you might drop by Tracey's and see what he has to say about that last set of lyrics I sent over by messenger this morning."

"The lyrics are your business," Lindsay told him curtly. "Drop by yourself."

15

OUT ON THE STREET Lindsay was ashamed of her loss of control. It wasn't Jonathon's fault that she felt locked in a box. But she'd had enough of music for one day, maybe for all time, and she stomped off in the icy air, determined not to think of anything that was even remotely related to sharps and flats and tonal passages.

When her temper had cooled a bit, she slowed down to look in the store windows, jostling in the crowds of last-minute shoppers that crowded the sidewalks. But as always, soon her thoughts drifted back to the winery.

At four o'clock in the afternoon what would Steven be doing? Walking in his plaid mackinaw through the woods? Poring over briefs in his book-lined study...talking to Rachel... joking with Clint?

Tomorrow was Christmas Eve. A crushing weight of sadness settled over her. How had the cranberries and the popcorn held up on the tree? Were the fir boughs on her mantel still crisp and green, or had Steven thrown them out?

Suddenly in front of her, in the middle of a

shop window, she saw the perfect gift for Steven. She pressed her face against the glass, feeling more alive and excited than she had for days. The object that attracted her attention was an ornament for a key chain. A tiny silver BMW. How exactly right! If she had combed the city, she could never have found anything more suitable, more certain to bring to Steven's lips the smile she adored.

Moving quickly, she had her hand on the doorknob before she remembered that a gift for Steven was an item she needn't be concerned about any longer. Stricken, she glanced back at the little charm, a perfect replica of the Old Gray Mare, right down to the sleepy enameled eyes that served as headlights. The charm had been made for Steven! But Steven was not on her Christmas list anymore.

She stood in the doorway of the shop and felt as if the buildings were crashing down on top of her. If Steven was no longer a part of her life, she had no life at all.

Music didn't matter. Nothing mattered except that she was miles from home. Miles from Steven's warm, protecting embrace, from the laughter in his blue eyes and the smell of his skin as he held her close.

Suddenly she broke out in a run. The persons nearest her stared and stepped quickly aside to make way for her. Panting, she raced down the block. Her cheeks grew rosy in the cutting wind, but she kept up her frantic pace until she reached the wine shop where Katie worked.

Katie was arranging a cheese display in the window. Pausing with a five-pound wheel of cheddar in her hand, she gaped through the glass at Lindsay, red-faced and breathless, beckoning for her to come out.

Ducking through the doorway, Katie asked fearfully, "What is it? What's happened?"

"I'm going home." Lindsay licked her parched lips. "Back to Terrapin Falls, back to the winery. I'm renting a car, I'm going now. Do you want to come?"

Katie blinked. "Of course I do. I've been wailing for days about spending Christmas away from mom and dad. But you said—"

"I know—that I couldn't spare the time." Lindsay tried to calm herself. "But I've just realized that nothing of importance will be going on here until after the holidays." Her thoughts raced to find a more plausible excuse. "I left some things at the cottage that I need. This seems the best time to get them."

Katie realized all at once that she was holding a wheel of cheese and that the proprietor was glaring at her through the window. She darted back inside with Lindsay following.

"What about it?" Lindsay whispered. "Do you want to come?"

Katie gave her an anguished look. "You know I do! But the shop isn't closing until noon tomorrow."

Lindsay let out her breath. "All right. We'll wait until then."

THE MILES PEELED AWAY under the wheels of the little rented Ford. With Katie chattering at her side, Lindsay reflected nervously on the step she had taken and what its consequences might be.

Waiting for Katie to get off work had seemed like an eternity, but at least it had given her a chance to make her explanations to Jonathon face-to-face. He'd been furious, of course.

"We cannot collaborate long-distance!" he had shouted after she'd made clear that she had no intention of returning from Connecticut.

"We will collaborate in that manner," Lindsay had told him, proud of her firmness, "or we will not collaborate at all."

But inside she'd been a quivering mass of uncertainty. Some of her excitement had worn off. She'd had time to remember that Steven had let her go without lifting a finger to stop her. He might be less than ecstatic when she turned up again on his doorstep. All she had to give her courage to risk it was that he had said if she ever needed him...if she ever wanted to come back....

Jonathon had stormed around his studio loft. "What kind of career do you think you'll have, stuck out there in the country?"

"Connecticut villages are full of writers and

painters and musicians, too," she'd replied spiritedly. She'd felt uncomfortably like Steven must have felt, listening to Jonathon speaking her own lines as he'd raged against what he'd called her stubborn foolishness.

"You haven't given New York a fair trial."

"I know that I can't compose here. I don't have to stay a month, or even another week, to find that out."

"You've done beautifully so far," he had insisted. "You'll adjust."

"So will you—to doing without me. Jonathon, look at this." She'd grabbed one of the songs she had brought with her from the farm, the song he had called a dandy. "This wasn't written in New York. I composed it and all the others in Connecticut without any encouragement from you, without the stimulation of hearing a producer praise me or the excitement of walking down Broadway. The music came out of my heart, Jonathon. And I'm going back where my heart functions best."

She had lifted a hand to silence fresh protests. "When I have the finale ready for you, I'll send it. Or bring it, if that suits you better. After that, we'll get together whenever we need to. But what you have to understand is that I can't live here!"

The truth was that she couldn't live without Steven. She could exist—maybe in time she could even put notes together again and call them songs. But away from Steven, she was certain at last, she would produce no music worth the name.

How incredible that she had been so slow in recognizing that truth when at the same time she was acutely aware of the fact that it was the passion and tenderness of his lovemaking that had unlocked her heart and set free that first haunting melody, the first composition of genuine merit that she had ever written. With Steven she was a whole person. He was her breath, the beat of her heart, the key to all the harmonies within her.

And she couldn't wait to tell him!

With growing excitement she pressed down on the accelerator of the Ford, picturing as Katie chattered, Steven's face when he saw her . . . imagining herself again in his arms. . . .

But in the holiday traffic, the journey stretched out endlessly. Night caught up with them long before Lindsay turned her headlights into the lane that led to the winery and to the cottage beyond where Katie's parents would in a moment be treated to their best Christmas surprise.

The closer the car came to the farmhouse, the more eagerly Lindsay peered ahead. All the way along the turnpike she had held fast to the hope that the windows would be glowing with the candles Steven had promised to have burning for her return. They had quarreled in the meantime, of course. But remembering Steven's desolate look when he said goodbye had enabled her to believe that whatever his reasons for letting her go, he did love and need her. Wouldn't he know intuitively that she was on her way, that as fast as she could she was covering the miles that separated them?

But the clapboard house was dark and forlorn among its trees when they reached it. As they passed by, Katie said with a quick glance at Lindsay's tense profile, "It looks as if Steven's gone off for the holiday."

"I'm not sure what his plans were," Lindsay managed to get out, but it was a struggle to keep her tears back. It couldn't be that she had come all this way to find him gone! Not when she was ready at last to arrange her life on Steven's terms, whatever they were. Fate wouldn't be cruel enough to deny her the joy of telling him that, would it?

But the dark house in the rearview mirror seemed to testify otherwise.

At Katie's house, Lindsay called out a hasty goodbye to the girl and her rejoicing parents and turned the car around. Heading back toward the winery, she thought numbly of Steven's betrayal. On this one night, for sentiment's sake at least, couldn't he have stayed at home? Her heart sank as she turned into his driveway. He might even have driven to Salem to be with his father.

But the Ford's headlights sweeping across the open garage showed the Old Gray Mare tucked snugly in her stable. With a pang, Lindsay recalled the silver charm that had been sold when she went back to buy it. If Steven had been at home, she wouldn't have had a gift to give him.

Then suddenly her spirits soared again. Steven might have lain down in the study for a nap before dinner. He often did. He could be there now, asleep, unaware that night had fallen!

Scrambling out of the car, she found the key to the front door in its customary place beneath a flowerpot. Rushing in, she flipped on the lights and raced upstairs. But the study was deserted. Picking her way quickly between piles of books toward a wadded afghan on the couch, she put her hands in the hollow that his body might have made. But it was as cold as the rest of the house, and she drew back, certain in her heart that he hadn't been there for days.

Still, she made a thorough desperate search of the place, calling Steven's name as she went. He had left plenty of tracks, she thought indignantly. Socks on the floor of the bedroom, an open bottle of shaving lotion in the bathroom. In the kitchen she found Dr. White on the table with Eleanor, half full of cold coffee.

But Steven himself was nowhere to be found.

Lindsay sat down dejectedly on the sofa in the parlor and stared with glazed eyes at the Christmas tree and the decorations she and

Steven had made. She looked at the unlit candles and the cold hearth.

At least she knew he hadn't gone as far as Annabelle's or he would have taken the car. He wasn't out stargazing because at dusk the sky had been leaden with snow clouds. That left the possibility that he might be somewhere in the neighborhood, somewhere he could be reached by phone! But she dismissed the thought of calling him as too humiliating after she had imagined a totally different reunion.

However, if he was in the neighborhood, perhaps it wasn't too late for an altered version of that reunion. If he was nearby, he would come home before long . . . and when he arrived. . . .

In the wood bucket she found some kindling and quickly started a glowing blaze. The crackle of the logs further lifted her spirits, and she hurried around the room, humming while she pulled back the homespun curtains and lighted the candles in the windows.

Then she rushed out to the kitchen. Digging around in Steven's wine closet, she found his prized bottle of Pouilly-Fumé and plunged it into a bucket of ice. Sure all at once that her preparations would act as a magnet to draw him home, she sat down to wait. But in minutes, she was up again, nervously setting the house to rights. As an hour ticked by, she washed and dried the dishes she found scat

tered in the kitchen, taking care to properly re-
place Eleanor and Dr. White on their shelf. She
straightened the upstairs. She leafed through a
magazine.

Finally at twelve o'clock, she blew out the
candles in the windows. Pressing her forehead
against the cold glass, she looked out into the
darkness.

"You're a fool, Lindsay Hancock," she whispered dismally. The past rose up to accuse her:
a failed marriage, blind alleys, dead ends, one
mistake after another. This time she had been
so sure . . . and this time she was wrong again.

Tear-blinded, she banked the fire and turned
out the lights. Her high hopes, her dreams of
pouring out her soul to Steven, seemed like lu-
natic fantasies when she was out again in the
icy air. In the week she had been away, she
reflected sadly, Steven had not tried once to
contact her. Why hadn't she taken her cue
from that? If he had cared at all, he would
have found out from Katie's parents where
she was staying.

One thing was certain. Wherever Steven
was tonight, he wasn't thinking of her.

Desolate, she crawled into her car, dreading
the idea of presenting herself at the inn at such
a late hour. With her hand poised on the igni-
tion, she thought longingly of her little cottage
just down the hill. Locked. And Steven had the
key.

But there was a window in the storeroom

that fit poorly, she remembered with a new rush of hope. A window low enough for her to climb through if she could pry it loose.

Captivated by the idea of having one more night in the cottage where she had found so much happiness, she tumbled out of the car again and started off down her favorite approach through the vineyard, oblivious to everything except salvaging the only kind of comforting homecoming that was left to her.

But halfway there, a chill crept up her backbone. She had never known a night to be so miserably dark. Even the rows of vines on either side had been swallowed up in the blackness. With a shiver she recalled the eerie sensation of going back to Christmas Church after the explosion. Every landmark had vanished. Where once a row of neat houses, hers among them, had stood, there was only an open field. Not a sign remained that a village had been there.

Panicked, Lindsay stopped still, clutching her overnight bag and trying to get her bearings. Which way was the cottage? Had it ever existed at all? Trembling, she listened to the wind.

Then all at once she sensed movement nearby. A twig snapped under someone's foot. A muffled gasp of terror ripped from her throat as a shadowy form stepped out in front of her. Then a familiar voice, thick with disbelief, rushed out at her. "Lindsay—is that you?"

"*Steven?*" Her bag hit the path with a thud as she hurled herself into his arms. "Oh—thank God!"

The world came back into focus. This was Steven, her darling Steven! All the dark thoughts from her hours of waiting scattered in the wind as he crushed her against his chest.

"You're back—" His arms locked around her. He buried his face in her hair. For one heavenly moment she was living out her most precious dream. Then suddenly she was aware that his embrace had loosened. He stepped away from her. "Why?" he asked tautly.

"What?" She strained to see his face through the darkness.

"Why did you come back? Did things go sour in New York?"

"Things went very well in New York!"

"Then what are you doing here?"

Lindsay tried to control her trembling. "Do I need a reason?"

"You have one, don't you?"

"As a matter of fact I do!" All the love she was ready to spill out trembled on her tongue. But if he hadn't guessed, if he didn't feel as she did, was there any point in telling him? Chin quivering, she tossed her hair back over her shoulder in the old defiant way. "I came to get some clothes I forgot. I've been freezing in New York."

He said in a voice that bore no resemblance

to the eager greeting he had given her, "It looks to me like you're freezing now." Abruptly he bent and picked up her bag from the path. "You'd better come with me to the house and warm up."

"I've been to the house," she said scathingly. "Nobody was there."

Steven said gruffly, "Rachel and Tom asked me to stop by. But if you had let me know you were coming—"

It's Christmas Eve! she wanted to shout. She had told him wild horses couldn't keep her away, but he had been too faithless—or hadn't cared enough—to light even one candle.

"I'll build a fire for myself in the cottage." She put out her hand. "Give me the key, please."

"Do you think I carry it around with me?"

"Never mind then!" She choked back her tears. "I meant to crawl through a window anyway."

"Don't be foolish, Lindsay."

"It won't be the first time!"

He gripped her arm firmly. "Come on with me. It's beginning to snow."

16

IN STONY SILENCE Steven pulled Lindsay along with him up the hill, but when they passed the rented car in the driveway, he questioned gruffly, "Is that yours?"

"Who else would it belong to?" she answered sullenly.

He fished the key from under the flowerpot. "I thought your friend Jonathon might have brought you."

"And where do you think he is? Sitting around in your dark old house?"

Steven unlocked the door. Fragrant warm air wafted out to greet them. He glanced around in surprise. "Somebody has been sitting around in my dark old house." Switching on the lights, he strode across the hall into the parlor where Lindsay's banked fire still glowed faintly. "Somebody who wears the same perfume as you."

Lindsay's face heated. "I waited a few minutes to see if you'd show up. I couldn't very well hang around in the cold, could I?"

He stared for a moment into the shimmer of

her smoky eyes. "I'm glad you had sense enough not to try."

Tossing down his mackinaw, he went to poke the fire. He seemed thinner, Lindsay thought with a pang. And infinitely weary.

"How is Katie?" he asked.

"I brought her home for the holidays. But she loves New York. She has a job and she won her audition hands down."

"So I've been told." He turned around with a wry grimace. "Her mother would like it announced hourly on television from Maine to Massachusetts."

Lindsay shifted her gaze. In New York she had ached for Steven's humor, but now she felt nothing but a terrible emptiness, remembering their quarrel. "You overreacted in regard to Katie."

"Perhaps I did." He stared hard at her. "Perhaps I did in other ways, too."

Lindsay's breathing quickened. But he turned back toward the fire. In a moment she commented formally, "The Christmas tree seems to be holding up well."

Steven gave it a sidelong glance. "It looks even better since somebody swept the dust out from under it."

Lindsay thrust her chin forward. "Sweeping helped to pass the time while you were dallying at Rachel's."

"As long as you were at it, there were a few

dirty dishes you could have washed up in the kitchen."

"A few! I don't think you've touched the place since I left."

He turned toward the kitchen abruptly. "Would you like a nightcap?"

"No, thank you." Then all at once she remembered the wine she had left chilling in the kitchen and jumped up from the sofa. "I'm warm now!" she called after him. "If you'll just give me the key to the cottage—"

But he was already out of hearing. Almost at once he was back again. "What," he asked quietly, "is this?"

Lindsay blanched, but she faced squarely what she had so festively prepared hours before. "It looks like a wine cooler and a bottle of wine."

"Not just any bottle." He set it down on the table next to the sofa. "It's the best Pouilly-Fumé in my closet." His penetrating gaze bored into her. "I was saving if for a celebration."

"Oh, were you!" Her eyes filled suddenly with the tears she had held back all evening. "Well, if you weren't such a mulish, blind, heartless person, *this* could have been a celebration!"

The tears spilled over and ran down her face. "Just for the record, I didn't come back here for clothes. I came to tell you that I made a discovery in New York."

Steven focused keenly on her. "What kind of discovery?"

"It doesn't matter now. But I'll tell you this. I've made a lot of foolish mistakes, but the most foolish one was falling in love with you, Steven Strake!" She swiped angrily at her tears. "Yes—I did sweep your floor and wash your dishes this evening! I picked up your socks, too, and straightened your messy study. And I had a lovely time doing it." A sob caught in her throat. "Can you guess why? Because I was silly enough to believe that sooner or later you'd come home to me . . . and naive enough to hope that you were in love with me too."

"Lindsay—" He took hold of her shoulders. "Listen a minute."

She tore his hands away. "Just give me the key to the cottage. In the morning I'll be gone. And I promise you this time I won't come back."

His jaw tightened. "You said you were in love with me."

Her voice shook. "I'll get over it."

"Do you want to, Lindsay?"

"More than anything else in the world!"

He said curtly, "The decision is yours, of course."

"Your stock answer to every crisis we've ever faced!"

He gazed at her steadily. "It always will be my answer. But this time, before you go, take a minute to listen to me first." Reaching out for his mackinaw, he pulled from a pocket the key she had asked for.

Lindsay gasped. "You had it with you all the time!"

His eyes raked over her. "The cottage should still be warm as toast. Rachel and Tom did ask me to their house as I told you. But I didn't go. I spent the evening sitting in your parlor on your bowlegged sofa." He paused, his eyes aglow with a strangely penetrating light. "I spent it wishing you were sitting there too."

"What?" Lindsay whispered.

"Yes. While you were waiting up here," he said thickly, "I was waiting down there. Not that I thought there was a chance you'd come. I gave up believing that days ago. But it was Christmas Eve." His voice hoarsened. "Better to spend it with half a dozen cardboard boxes that belonged to you than with no part of you at all."

"Oh, Steven—" Half crying, half laughing, Lindsay flew into his arms. "Do you know what you're saying?"

He gathered her to him. "What I should have said weeks ago. I love you. Oh, Lindsay, I love you."

He crushed her against him as he had done in the vineyard, but this time there was no pulling away. "I was so sure you hadn't come back because of me that I was afraid even to ask what you were doing down there on the path. A whole week, an eternity, and not a word from you, not a sign that you felt as I do."

"If you tell me you love me a hundred times," she moaned, "I'm not sure I'll believe you. Do you know how I've ached to hear those words? Oh, Steven—" She caught his face between her hands and brought his lips to hers. "What held you back? What kept you from telling me?"

He groaned between her kisses. "It's a long story, darling."

"We have the rest of the night."

"Let's not waste it talking."

HE MADE LOVE to her in front of the fire where they had first lain down together. The ardent possessive way he undressed her and the perfect, powerful thrusts of his body as he claimed her assured Lindsay that he had hungered for her deeply. Her own passionate response was equally intense. Their arching, shuddering climb to fulfillment ended in the kind of exquisite release Lindsay had wept for in her rented room in New York, and she clung to Steven in joyous surrender until both of them were spent and panting.

But when they lay back with the heat of desire still a smoky haze around them, Lindsay yearned to know what the future held. When Steven's breathing had slowed she asked quietly, "Where do we go from here?"

"Impatient wench," he chided softly, but his hardened palms roved lovingly over the sheen of her back. "Can't we enjoy one delight at a time?"

"If you're sure there are more delights ahead."

His gaze grew solemn. "Are you sure, Lindsay, that you want there to be?"

In answer, she gave him a long, lingering kiss.

Steven sighed. "Have I ever mentioned how lovely you are?"

"Not nearly often enough."

"Do you know how much I missed you?"

"It may take you weeks to tell me properly."

He raised himself on one elbow and touched a finger to her lips. "But in the meantime we have serious matters to discuss. Is that what you're thinking?"

"More or less."

He ducked his head into the hollow of her throat and kissed her greedily. "Let's have more of this and less of the other."

For another few minutes she was content with his lighthearted play. She sank her teeth gently into one of his earlobes and then tickled him until he begged for mercy. He blew in her ear and growled alarmingly between her breasts. Then all at once, play turned into passion. Ignited, they fell back, limbs entangled, moaning out their pleasure in the exquisite, tumultuous friction of flesh against flesh.

But at last Steven sat up and brought her up beside him. He laid his hands on her naked shoulders, then drew them slowly down to her wrists.

"Now," he said, fixing her with his steady gaze, "tell me what you discovered in New York."

But she shook her head. "You first. What did you discover here?"

He hesitated. "That I'd gambled on your return and lost."

"But you didn't lose!"

He got up and went to the sofa and brought an afghan back. He draped it around them, and then he and Lindsay turned toward the fire.

"I'm about to give you a bit of history, Lindsay. Mine. You may yawn if you like, but don't go to sleep."

"Steven, stop teasing me!"

He dropped a few whispery kisses along her hairline. "I'm stalling, that's what I'm doing."

"Why?"

"Because looking back on the last few months, and especially on the last week, it scares me to realize what a fine line I was walking and how dangerously close to the edge of the precipice." His voice roughened. "If you hadn't come back—"

"Darling, you're not making any sense."

He sighed. "The straight facts then. Are you ready?"

She snuggled closer.

He began. "Three years ago when I started thinking of leaving the law firm, I wrote to one of my sisters, to Katherine—my favorite—and told her what was on my mind." He chuckled wryly. "I might as well have dropped a bomb at the Sunday school picnic."

"She didn't approve?"

"She thought I was insane. She knew how hard I'd worked to get my law degree. She kept asking me, 'How can you throw all that away to make *wine*?' She couldn't believe I'd even consider anything so ridiculous. And neither could my other three sisters when she'd spread the word. Or my father, either."

Lindsay looked up at him sympathetically. "Was there a great hue and cry?"

Steven smiled grimly, remembering. "There were lamentations and sackcloth. They looked at me as if I'd died. They kept reminding me that I was the only lawyer our branch of the family had ever produced. No one was amused when I pointed out that we'd never had a winemaker in the family either. They were so disappointed in me. They'd been so proud and now I was about to disgrace them by acting a fool just when I'd made something out of myself."

"Poor Steven," Lindsay murmured. "You must have felt terrible."

"I was feeling terrible enough trying to cope with my own doubts and the flak I was getting at the office. With my family's piled on top of it, it was a lot to handle."

He was quiet for a time, staring into the fire. "The hardest thing of all was that they loved me. If it hadn't been for their love I could have shrugged off their objections."

"But you loved them, too," Lindsay said. "You wanted to please them."

He nodded. "My sisters had all mothered me. I was my father's only son. I was letting them down when what I wanted was to make them happy. But I finally realized, when I was thinking of jumping off the Triboro Bridge," he joked grimly, "that nobody can make anyone else happy by playing false with himself."

Lindsay nodded. "That's true, isn't it. If you'd stayed on in New York and tried to make yourself into what they wanted you to be, after a while you would have become the kind of man none of them would have respected. Then they would have been angry that you'd let them make up your mind for you when you were the one whose responsibility it was to decide what was best."

"Yes." He gave her a long look. "That's it exactly."

Lindsay waited for him to go on. But after a moment she swung her head around slowly. "What you've been telling me is that if you had tried to hold me here with your love, you would have been doing the same thing to me that your family did to you."

He nodded solemnly. "There were so many times when it was all I could do to keep from telling you how much I loved you, how much I needed you to make my life complete. But I had to let you go, Lindsay, free and unencumbered, to discover whether or not there was room for me, for the farm and for your music, too, in your life. I had to gamble that if you loved me, you'd find a way to make it all work and come back. And if you couldn't, I had to face it and let you go."

"That's what you were doing tonight down at the cottage," she whispered. "Letting me go."

"Yes." He brushed back a lock of her shining hair. "Next to saying goodbye to you the morning you left, it was the hardest thing I've ever done. It would have been so easy to call you or go to New York and beg you to come back. Then there you were all at once on the path. It was like a miracle, a miracle I couldn't trust until I saw the wine cooling in the kitchen, and then I knew."

Lindsay slipped her hands up around his neck and laid her cheek against his chest. "What a wonderful Christmas gift! The freedom always to follow my heart, no matter where it leads me."

He took her arms down and kissed the insides of her wrists. "There's one problem still unresolved," he said huskily. "You made your decision to come back, but Broadway is still there. The lights are still glittering, the curtains are still rising on the musicals you have the talent to write the scores for. What are you going to do about that?

"Write the scores," she said softly.

His brows drew together in a troubled frown.

Lindsay smoothed it away with loving fingers. "My discovery was that my inspiration isn't New York, my darling. It's you. I don't need glittering lights or clever producers to make music." She brought her lips to his. "All I need is you. Are you going to let me stay?"

"You funny nut," he grinned. "Just try to get away."

"You haven't proposed."

"I want to propose a toast when I do." He got to his feet and pulled her up. Looking down at her with smoldering eyes, he said, "Let's dress and then we'll drink to Mr. and Mrs. Steven Strake of Terrapin Falls, Connecticut."

Lindsay's hands trembled as she pulled on her clothes. "I'll bring the glasses," she said as Steven lifted the wine bottle from the cooler.

But in the kitchen her unsteady fingers knocked a cup and saucer out of the cabinet as she reached for the goblets. Steven heard her gasp and then came the sound of china crashing on the floor.

"What's going on?" he called out from the parlor. "Is there a mutiny among the crockery?" When there was no response, he strode out to see what was the matter.

Lindsay stood white-faced over the remains of Eleanor and Dr. White.

"Look what I've done," she said in a muffled whisper.

Steven glanced down at the broken bits and put his arm around her. "Sad," he said and kissed her gently. "But not the end of the world."

"Steven, it's an awful omen." She lifted eyes brimming with tears. "Eleanor and Dr. White have presided over so many of our special occasions. They were a talisman. And now to have shattered them just as we're planning a new life together—" She shuddered.

Steven reached down for a fragment of the dainty Haviland demitasse. Turning to Lindsay he said hoarsely, "In my more optimistic moments I considered going into Terrapin Falls and buying you a ring. Now I know what kept me from it." He took her hand in his and onto her ring finger he slipped Eleanor's tiny, flowered handle.

"Will you marry me, Lindsay?"

"Oh, Steven! Oh, my darling—yes!"

They embraced for a long, lingering kiss. Then Steven took her by the hand and led her to the window. "Look," he said. "There's your gift to me."

The black night that had frightened her so was gone, she saw. Morning had come, Christmas morning, filled with a dazzling blizzard of snowflakes.

"How beautiful," she breathed. "But I don't understand. What have I given you?"

"Heaven, my love." He put his arms around her. "Can't you see? All my stars are falling down."

THE AUTHOR

When she is not writing romance novels or short stories, Meg Dominique may be found birdwatching, gardening, or taking her daily four-mile hike. She also enjoys traveling, which often provides ideas for her stories. *When Stars Fall Down* came about after a visit to a Connecticut winery.

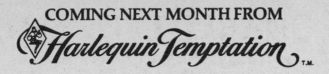